The Sin of You

Absinthe

This book is suitable for **adult audience**. It contains sexually explicit scenes and graphic language which may be considered offensive by some readers.

I advise you to take a deep breath and prepare to be seduced by dark forces.

Golden letters

Sarah

I'm standing in the middle of a strange room. Every object surrounding me seems to tell its own story. The faded cracking of the furniture from time to time sends shivers down my spine, giving me a weird feeling of restlessness. Must be from the faint smell of cologne that remained in the air, leaving small pieces of endorphins to play with my senses.

The sound of a closing door lets me know that he's here. My body instantly melts, responding to his unspoken calling. A hand approaches me, but I can't see anything more since the rest of his figure is covered by darkness.

A strand of my hair is pulled aside and his fingers make contact with my skin.

I wonder every time how such a cold touch can emanate so much heat and in seconds strip me of everything that I considered mine and make it his own. I know so well what's going to happen next, how his strong arms are going to pull me closer, letting me feel every inch of his body while resting upon his chest. As expected he does just that, and even though I saw it coming, the power of his presence never ceases to amaze me.

My eyes close instinctively, letting the pleasure of him run through my every pore.

One of his hands is tangled in my hair, slowly pulling my head to the side in order to gain access to the exposed skin of my neck. I can feel his breathing become deeper, taking a moment to enjoy the newly discovered sight. Just moments left until he can claim me as his. He pulls me closer and I can feel all his muscles tense as his lips make contact with the soft warm skin of my neck, leaving a trail of goosebumps in their path.

Seconds after, I feel his teeth grazing my skin. I open my eyes, eager to see the one who managed to erase all my previous existence in just a few seconds from his first touch.

And then it happens...

The darkness evaporates as once more light finds its way in, making the room an all too familiar place. It was just a dream. The same dream that has haunted my every night for almost two years now. Small drops of sweat are resting on my forehead reminding me how my existence is ruled by something I have never known... An illusion that disappears as the first rays of light reach my sheets, leaving me empty and yearning for a fantasy that will never happen.

I finally decide to leave my bed, even though I wished so hard to close my eyes in order to find out how my dream would end. But I've tried that before, on a hundred different mornings, without being able to feel his bittersweet touch on my skin. My feet fell heavily to the floor, entangled in the sheets as I forced myself to go get ready for work.

I actually love my job! It gives me great satisfaction, but sometimes I dream of living in another kind of world, where the passion I put into my work would also reflect in my private life. I graduated from art school first in my class. That was a year and a half ago and ever since then I've been working for an art gallery as an assistant.

I usually track down art pieces from different collectors, trying to negotiate a decent price so that we can make a good profit selling them. I really love the detective vibe that this gives me, but since I'm a newbie, the jobs I'm given aren't of such great importance. I'm starting to feel more like a scavenger hunter than a real art dealer.

Can't complain about the paycheck though. New York is an expensive city and being able to afford a decent apartment along with the ability to dress in a few pieces of designer clothes is more than enough for now.

I quickly pull my hair up into a ponytail, slip into a tight black skirt, grab a white dress shirt, a pair of heels and I'm out the door.

My boss is usually understanding, but the lack of promptness is a deal breaker for her. Forcing my luck I signal for a cab, and amazingly, I manage to get a taxi driver to pull over in the middle of rush hour. Another day in which I was able to make it work on time.

I place a coffee I bought from across the street on my boss's desk, then go to sit at the small table that's supposed to be *'my office'*. Strange that she's not in yet. She usually arrives before all of us do.

"Sign Here" A courier pulls me away from my thoughts handing me a small envelope.

"Is this what I think it is?" My boss, Karla pulls at the folded paper eager to open it.

I didn't even see her come in... What is wrong with me today? I am in desperate need of some normal sleep!

"Oh, yes! I've been waiting a long time for this to arrive," she happily exclaimed while waving the piece of paper in front of me.

"This is our ticket to Manhattan!" she smirked handing me back the paper. "Mr. Bechard requests the pleasure of your company at the annual Fall Gala that will take place on the 5th of October," the *golden letters* shined against the ivory sheet.

"I think I've heard of Mr. Bechard before... Isn't he some kind of successful businessman?" I asked Karla.

"Yes, he is. But even though he has more money than Gates himself, he's not our main target. His taste in art is poor. He'd rather spend millions on some new artist's piece than buy something of real historical value. Some of the people who will attend the event are of much greater interest."

"Every one of you will be assigned a specific person to try and get to work with our gallery, as a client or a seller."

"This, my dear, is your chance to prove yourself! To step up on the food chain and hopefully make it as a manager." These words lingered in my ears for a while, making me wish for it more. A manager's position would give me the freedom to search for valuable art pieces, not just for bits and scraps in some old lady's house.

"Your interest should focus on Damien Arion. A very intriguing young man if I might say. Even though my charms haven't failed me yet, I am a little old for seducing my way into his pocket." Karla pouted. "He is known for his discrete nature and for the beautiful young ladies that are seen on his arm at different events."

"Rumor has it that he owns impressive art collections scattered across his properties. Amongst his artifacts I believe there is said to be a Shang Dynasty vase that sold in private bidding 10 years ago for the sum of 1.5 million dollars. That single vase is now worth $10 million if you know the right buyer... And it just so happens that I do."

"So, I don't care what you do... threaten him, seduce him... even marry the guy... I just want a way into his house and for him to take a seat at a negotiation table to discuss business."

I need that manager's position, and no man is going to stand in my way!

"I guess I'll have to find a really short dress then."

Sweet dream

A knock on the door steals me away from my dream. His passionate lips didn't get to touch my skin this time as I awoke to the daily torture that I call my real life. I barely manage to get out of bed and find my way through the living room to see who had the audacity to bother me this early on a Saturday morning.

The door opens and I am greeted by the presence of a person I know so well... Too well if you ask me. Lala as I call her from childhood, or Laura by her real name. She is my oldest and dearest friend, except for this morning when I could easily have thrown her back in the street for waking me. We practically grew up together in Philadelphia but we decided to move to NY, mostly to escape our parents and to gain the so much wanted independence.

"Wake up!"

"I'm standing, so I'm up!" I muttered giving her an annoyed look.

"Not with that face you're not! Did I interrupt your date with Prince Charming?"

I can't handle her this morning...

"Hey! Don't walk away from me!" Lala shouted as I made my way to the kitchen to get a much-needed cup of coffee. Her words were echoing around the room but the sound of the coffee filter was much sweeter than her babbling this morning. Drop by drop my mug filled with its precious liquid and after only a few sips the world around me started to make sense.

"Lala, isn't it a little early for this visit? What are you doing here at 7 am?"

"Haven't you been listening to a word I said?"- to my amusement her eyes almost popping out of her head. "I can't processes without coffee." I shrugged, letting my body slip into one of the kitchen chairs.

She slowly passed by me to get herself a cup "I came here to get you to go clubbing."

"At 7 am? Have you lost your mind?"

"Tonight, not now... I was on my way to work and I just thought I'd stop by and ask you."

"Texts... Ever heard of them?" I muttered under my breath trying to figure out how it is that she's still my friend. She threw her arms around me and gave me a huge hug "Ahhh... Bestie, I thought I'd share the pleasure of waking up this early on a weekend day."

"So thoughtful of you, but I'll have to pass on the clubbing this time. My boss wants me to seduce a guy into working with us."

"Did you switch jobs and I'm not aware of it?" Her reaction made me smile as I realized what Karla was really asking me to do at the gala. "There's this guy... Damien Arion. I have to convince him to work with our gallery."

Lala's eyes widened as she slowly put her cup on the kitchen counter. Then she broke out into hysterical laughter... "Damien... You need to seduce Damien into working with you?"

"Would you stop laughing and tell me what's so amusing?" I pouted and crossed my arms. I knew that my reaction would make her stop and actually explain things to me, without having to deal with a half an hour of her making jokes.

"Jeeezzz! I thought you had an active social life with all those events you organize for work."

"Let me enlighten you a little, cause by the look on your face you have no idea who you're dealing with."

"Spit it out already"- I grumbled, already exhausted by the pressure this day was threatening to put on me.

"Damien Arion, one of the most discrete and desirable bachelors in the Big Apple, has made another conquest. He was seen two days ago accompanied by a beautiful red-head entering the building in which his 27 million dollar apartment is located.

You could only imagine what happened next.

But don't worry ladies, his private life doesn't interfere with his conquests, and at the speed he switches his women, there's always room for more."

"What's that supposed to mean?" I asked confused after hearing her recite those words as a weird poem.

"That was a Vogue quote... and I personally would add.... there's always room for more if you're a beautiful model...because those are the women they're referring to"- Lala put her hands on her hips, probably proud of memorizing that whole article.

"I'm not sure what I should be more concerned about, me having no chance of getting him to work with us, or the fact that you recited a whole article about the guy, without even blinking?"

"If you'd seen the guy, you'd memorize the very air he breathes."

"Wait... I'll search for a photo online."

"No! I don't want to jinx it!" I pushed her phone away, mostly because I was scared by the fact that if he was too good looking I would get nervous. The truth is that this is a very big deal for me. In just one evening I could get at least a couple of years closer to my chance of being a manager, without all the unnecessary ass-kissing of my boss. I didn't have any intention of seducing the guy, but a nice dress and good makeup can sometimes get you closer to your goal.

"Hey, did I lose you again?"...Lala brought me back from my thoughts.

"No... I just don't know what to wear tonight." Her eyebrows frowned like she was processing a lot of information in just a few seconds "Definitely not a short dress!"

"I was actually thinking about a short dress."

"You're going to a gala, not a cocktail party. I was expecting you to know better than this." Her index finger was running through the air just like a teacher scolding a student that didn't pay attention in class. "That doesn't mean you can't be sexy... We'll compensate for the short dress with a long, but cut open one... And a very generous cleavage."

"I know your conception of a very generous cleavage and I'm definitely not going with that... A medium cleavage is more than enough for me. Anyway, not all men want everything out in the open."

"Those are exactly the words of a woman that doesn't have anything to put out in the open, but hun, that's not your case. Anyway, you were going for a short dress a few moments ago."

"You need class and sass!" She was taking the last drop of my energy away with every word she spoke.

"Aren't you late for work or something like that?" I asked her, desperate to get back into my bed. I'm really not a lazy person, but working 10 hours a day during the week takes its toll. I usually use the weekends to recharge my batteries to be ready for the working week to come.

"I'm leaving...I don't like you this early in the morning anyway... Just be careful tonight ... Or don't be!" Lala chuckled grabbing her bag, then headed out the door. "I'll let myself out ... Love you!"

"Love you too, crazy!" I yelled loud enough for her to hear me, forgetting that my neighbors were probably still sleeping at this time. I looked at my coffee mug, then searched around the room, confused as to what my plans for the day should be. I'll have to go shopping for a dress and even though I don't like admitting it, Lala's suggestion was pretty good.

But for now, the perfect plan seems to be to get back to bed and spend a few more hours cuddling up between my silk sheets. I still have hopes that I would meet the Prince of Darkness in my sleep again, but the *sweet dream* unfortunately never appears during the daytime. So I close my eyes and fantasize about his lips traveling my skin, reaching the places he never manages to until the break of dawn.

Night lights

"This is it!" I tell myself whilst standing in front of the mirror, rearranging my new dress.

Yes, I followed Lala's advice and bought a long black dress with a generous cut on the side. A few loose curls, a little makeup, a pair of Louboutin's and the night can begin. I'm not sure why I'm stressing out about this because I usually have things my own way. As for the times that I don't, well I work on it until I do.

Tonight isn't going to be any exception.

Karla actually sent a car to collect me which is a little unusual for her. Even though she pays us very well for what we do, she tries to save on any additional expenses, *"cut the losses"* is how she likes to call it. A cheapass... is what I really think.

My phone vibrated, letting me know that my ride arrived. I left the apartment with a light heart, like something was calling me to a different place. Even though I was nervous about tonight, I was also excited. This evening my life might change forever. I'll be damned if I'll let anything stand in my way! The night had a certain magic to it. As I traveled to my destination the city lights seemed to shine a little brighter, making me appreciate the beauty of darkness.

The car pulled up at the foot of the red carpet. The paparazzi flashes started to twinkle outside the car's windows. They soon came to an end as they realizing that I was no one of great importance to them. I breathed out, relieved that I escaped any unwanted attention. I do want success, but in my line of work seeing my face in some useless tabloid is definitely not on my to-do list.

I made my way through the lobby and entered the biggest room I have ever seen. Hundreds of people were gathered under the same roof. I realized that finding Karla or any of my co-workers was going to be a tough mission.

My eyes set on the bar. The thought of having a small drink to release a little of my stress was very appealing. It was easier said than done. On my way to my first destination of the night, a hand from the crowd grabbed me, forcing me to stop walking. I turned around and my face came within inches of a white dress shirt. I was forced to look up at the stylishly dressed man who was so much taller than me.

He was a sight for sore eyes!

A perfect Tom Ford tuxedo that let half an inch of his dress shirt out in the open made it obvious that this man had both good taste and money. His mysterious hazel eyes, complemented by a seductive smile made him irresistible to almost all woman-kind... except for me. Even though I'm absolutely sure every lady in this room was craving to be in his presence, he just wasn't my type.

"You finally came!" he smirked while brushing his bottom lip with his tongue.

"I'm not sure I know you, let alone that you were expecting me!" I chuckled. The truth was that although I didn't know him, I definitely knew who he was. Augusto Piero, a young Italian businessman who made a small fortune from some online sporting goods shops. I wished his taste in art would match the one he has for clothes. Unfortunately, I remember reading an article in the past about him having spent a huge sum of money on some paintings that I wouldn't hang in my bathroom not even if they paid me.

However, money is money in whatever form. Maybe I could get him to spend some of his in our gallery.

"I haven't had the pleasure of being introduced, but I didn't lie when I said that I was expecting you. I've had a feeling that tonight I'd be honored by the presence of a beautiful young lady, such as yourself. But let me properly introduce myself. My name is Augusto Piero, a modest entrepreneur," he smirked again. At this point I was more than sure that I recognized his face from the newspapers.

Two can play at this game! "I am Sarah Edison, art dealer." I chuckled crossing my arms and giving him my best Bamby look.

"I have a high interest in all things beautiful. Art will always have a special place in my heart," his tongue was once again trailing his bottom lip as soon as he finished speaking.

I wasn't sure where my boss was. I kept looking over his shoulder from time to time, trying to locate her. One thing I knew for sure, if I managed to get him to make a purchase from the gallery it would definitely smooth things out in case of a refusal from Mr. Arion. I'm really not sure how to get him out of the eyefucking vibe he is currently sending me and into a business frame of mind.

"Here you are my dear," Karla came between us right on time, giving me an idea on how to approach this.

"I was on my way to meet you when I stumbled on Mr. Piero. He was just telling me how art represents a great interest to him."

"Mr. Enzo, this is Karla Patrick, my employer."

He wasn't a man who easily gave up on his ambitions. He made an attempt to get rid of the new unwanted company "It seems we have a lot in common, but tonight I'm leaning towards some moments of relaxation. If I may be permitted, I'd like to take Ms. Edison out onto the balcony for a breath of fresh air."

"On any other occasion I'd be more than happy to let you steal her away, but tonight we are actually here on business. So, unfortunately, you will have to finish this conversation another time," Karla cut him short, visibly unimpressed by his potential value to the company and probably also by his taste of art.

"A couple of women dedicated to their work. I respect that! If your business meeting gets cut short, I'll be around." He nodded his head respectfully as he lost himself in the crowd "Have a pleasant evening ladies!"

To my surprise Karla was giving me a displeased look. "What were you doing talking to him? I thought I've made it perfectly clear that we were here on business."

"You made it perfectly clear, but he stopped me on my way to find you. I thought that I'd take a chance and see if I could convince him to be our client." I shrugged, a little surprised by her strong reaction. Under normal terms, landing a client such as Augusto would definitely put a smile on her face.

"He is not the one I'm interested in. Not tonight. We have bigger fishes to catch!" Her eyes traveled my body from head to toes checking out my outfit. "At least we know that you can get the attention of an attractive bachelor" she muttered rearranging my cleavage. "Let's see how you do with Damien... Don't forget, I need him to work with us!"

"I know... I know. He will land me the manager's position," I said to her. I was a little annoyed by her insistence on me working with this guy.

"Then you better get prepared to go up the ladder, because there he is," she grinned pointing to the corner of the room. "The one talking to that blond woman with the dark blue dress," Karla added.

Somehow I knew without her specifying the last part. My eyes were already set on him since the moment she pointed me in that direction. My breath almost stopped and a knot formed instantly in my stomach.

This most exquisite man was standing in the same room as me. Every single one of his features was perfect, just like he had come out of a beautiful painting that I could spend days studying. Piercing emerald green eyes, carefully arranged ebony hair and a neck tattoo that was peaking from under his collar was making me lose myself in this spectacular view. There was something about him. A special aura that made his darkness shine across the room. An invisible bond that drew me to the place he stood without me even moving my feet.

If I had any doubt in my mind that this man would change my life, all suspicions were washed away at my first sight of him. I knew that from this moment on *nothing will ever be the same again.*

First one last time

My heart never beat this fast before as my feet carried me towards the corner of the room where he stood. With every inch that separated us closing, my body betrayed me. My face started burning and a weird sensation was building up in my lower abdomen.

Hold it together! I told myself. I shook my head a little to remove all these new sensations that were taking control of my being. I'm a very strong person and I have no intention of showing Mr. Arion otherwise, even though I can hardly control my emotions as I approach him. The closer I came, the more his scent invaded all my senses, making my every breath occur only by the thought of him.

Every single person in the room simply evaporated, there was just me and him, alone, facing each other at the edge of time.

"Would you like a drink?" The voice of a waiter snapped me out of my newly found parallel world.

"I... Yes, please!" I breathed taking a glass of champagne, letting Damien's presence settle in the rest of my body. Being bold has always been my leverage, but right now even a simple hello seems to stumble on my lips.

"You're staring!" A harsh voice echoed in my ears, while the ink carved on his neck came to life as he spoke.

My eyes widened even more "That was definitely not my intention, Mr. Arion." I'm not sure how I managed to get the whole sentence out without babbling. Once I did, I felt so proud of myself that I was only one step away from thinking someone should give me an award for pulling through that.

"Could you let me know then what your intentions are Mrs..."

"Edison... Sarah Edison. I work in the art field, antiques to be precise. Knowing about your love of art, I'm very sure that we have some common ground," I whispered seductively, giving him my sexiest smile. But, contrary to all my beliefs, he gave me a more than displeased look "I hate to disappoint, but tonight my common ground is reserved for my company," he muttered while he moved his eyes to the woman standing next to him.

"I apologize for bothering you, our conversation would have been brief. I can assure you that my intentions weren't to deprive this young lady of your presence." Next thing I know his eyes turned black, letting his darkness surface. He blinked and shook his head in discomfort while muttering under his breath... "Please go, now!"

But it was too late...my eyelids felt heavy for a second and the lips of the mysterious man were vivid illusions on my skin. My sight clouded and Damien's all too familiar presence pushed me to the edge of my sanity.

Who is this man?

I didn't realize what was happening to me since he didn't move an inch... All I knew was that I had to get out of there before I totally lost all sense of reality. Gathering all my strength, I turned on my heels and started walking back to where I had come from, but not before I noticed him leaving the room, quickly followed by the woman who had accompanied him.

~~~

Damien

It was becoming hard for me to function properly. My inner beast was summoned the instant she entered the room. This hadn't happened to me in centuries and I was more than surprised by it. An uncontrollable lust was emerging inside of me, the sound of her blood running through her veins became like a mermaid's song, luring me to the point of losing all control.

I wasn't sure why, but I knew where the young woman was going. She was heading towards me, as the power of destiny was set upon our lives. This woman... This woman that was approaching me was the one in my dreams. A perfect black dress was covering her hourglass sinner body, alluring me with every single step she took, turning a king into a slave.

She was here.

The movement of her lips was making it almost impossible for me not to claim them as mine for all eternity. The intense urge of trailing kisses down her neckline was forcing me to oscillate between reality and fantasy. My human part wanted to touch her and the monster inside me craved to devour her.

Her presence was both heaven and hell. With every second that passed between us, my inner voice was pushing me to have her.

"Please go, now!" I managed to speak these words with the last drop of self-control left.

Fortune was on my side tonight as she did just that... A few seconds after my command, she obeyed and headed back on the path she had initially followed here. A second after her first step I felt my fangs betraying me as they were fighting to emerge. I had to get out of here. I pursued the dim light of a hallway and made my way into an empty staff room.

Before I managed to pull the door after me a woman's hand stopped it. Helen, my companion for the night, made her way into the room twisting the door key to secure our intimacy. Although she was beautiful, she was hideous compared to the woman I've just met.... the whole world faded compared to her.

I leaned hard on the desk sat in the middle of the room in my despair to silence the beast, but the sound of cracking wood filled the room as my palms unwillingly crushed the table top.

"Loosen up", Helen whispered seductively, kneeling in front of me and starting unbuckling my pants with lightning speed. Normally this would have been a great start to a promising evening, but I found myself taking a step back, causing her to almost fall on her face.

She didn't seem so enticing any longer, even though I never deprive myself of a beautiful woman's company... they make the time pass easier and since all my feelings are much more intense than those of normal people, lust makes no exceptions. On the contrary, it showed her face in different forms.

"Stand!" I commanded menacingly. She didn't fail to comply.

She must have misinterpreted my intentions because the moment she was up on her feet her lips made contact with my jawline and her hands were unbuttoning my shirt. Her need for me was increasing at the same pace as my frustration was building. The faded murmur that was leaving her lips while she was exploring new inches of my skin was now annoying me, sending me close to my breaking point.

My hand found her neck and, in a flash, pinned her to the wall across the room, slamming her body into the wall. She whimpered in discomfort, but shortly after she lifted one of her legs to my waist, letting my body come between them in her final attempt to reach her goal. Her eyes were full of desire as I removed a strand of hair that was hanging in front of her cleavage, uncovering her perfectly round breasts that were peaking from under the gown.

I needed her, but not in the way that she needed me. I tangled my hand in her hair, letting my fangs enter her flesh six or seven inches below her collarbone, right above her dress. She started whining to my enchantment. I was feeding more on her pain than on her blood itself since my endorphins weren't reaching her circulatory system fast enough to calm her despair.

I tried to concentrate on my little game, but my thoughts were already running towards Sarah and the need for blood was uncontrollable.

With the hand intertwined in her hair, I maneuvered her head like a puppeteer, tilting it to the side to gain access to her neck. My fangs retracted themselves from her chest and perforated the skin of her neck, finding the vein that would satisfy my appetite faster. Sip after sip I drank her, trying to find a certain sweetness in her blood, but there was none. The volume satisfied my hunger, but the taste left all my other senses on the edge, making me realize that nothing would fully please me from now on, except the alluring taste of Sarah's blood.

I managed to stop before I drained her "Go home, you can't show up back at the party like this." I did not want or need her presence any longer, even though most of the men at the gala would kill to have an hour alone with her. She bowed her head, listening to my command, as thousands like her had before and thousands more to follow would. A simple slave of my desires who will soon be replaced in my faded attempts to find satisfaction.

It took a moment of solitude to regain my composure, pushing back the beast and letting my human part settle in. I was clearly not prepared for tonight and soon I must leave because I'm still not sure of my power of self-control.

But my feet can't carry me away from this place, not without getting a glimpse of her for *one last time.*

Forever in a moment

I'm calmer now. My senses have slowly accustomed to her smell that was just floating throughout the whole building, but still, I have to leave. I abandoned the service room and made my way back to the main room where the gala was being held. My eyes needed to feast on the sight of her *just one last time*. It is a very dangerous thing for me to do, but I just can't help myself. My mind in its current delusional state actually thinks that holding a visual image of her in my memory can last me an eternity while my actual needs are far greater than that.

Every fiber of my being is begging me to take her to my bedroom and not to hold back until the clothes she is wearing are but pure memories strewn over the floor and I'm buried deep inside her. I wouldn't normally hesitate a second, but the longing to drink of her wouldn't have even let me reach my car. She would have been dead the instant we left this room.

For centuries I've managed to control my outbursts and with the passing of time has come the wisdom of self-control. Even if my nature is a rebellious one, my instinct of survival taught me that the seconds you take to think things through rather than acting on pure instinct can make the difference between life and death.

Still, no rational thinking was enough to make me leave without getting one more glimpse of her. As I entered the room I didn't need to search for where she was. All my senses were already screaming out, alerting me as to her exact location.

My gaze shifted to the bar where she was talking to another man. I recognize him immediately. Augusto, an overnight success story, a wealthy man who essentially thinks that all women should bow in front of him since he has more than enough dollars in his bank account and some fading good looks.

I had the misfortune to meet him at a party once where he has the audacity to approach one of my dates. Let's just say it didn't end well for him since I broke his hand in the bathroom. The only thing that kept me from ending his life there was the fact that the party was being held in one of my oldest friends' houses and I didn't want to cause a stir. Besides, my date thinking that I was in fact defending her honor, not my pride, decided to repay me quicker than I was planning... Like fucking her on a rooftop would leave her with much *honor...*

But this time it was very different. A rising warm sensation was surrounding my body and my cold blood seemed to be boiling.

I could see from her gestures that she was a little uncomfortable. The man was touching her arm with his one hand, whilst the fingers of his other hand rearranging a loose strand of hair under her ear. My jaw clenched and the blood within my veins started to pulse with an increasing rhythm. This was no longer about pride. This was now only *the pure lust to kill.*

He will not be leaving this party alive.

I focused only on what they were saying. I caught hold of the moment where he began opening an invitation to his bedroom.

"I can say that I pride myself on the art pieces that I've collected over the last couple of years. Over time I have managed to put together a remarkable collection. Since your boss is set on turning this night into a business one, I could offer you a private tour of my house for you to decide whether we can work together." He was talking so close to her cheek that I was already imagining myself ripping his head out in the middle of the room.

Unfortunately, I couldn't kill him right here. I do have certain powers of persuasion, but they are not strong enough to convince around 500 people to forget his blood splattering across the room. She was trying to let him down gently without blowing the deal, but the miserable look on her face was betraying her.

She was definitely not like other women. Even though much smaller than mine, his wallet would be enough to charm most of the females I know and with the inclusion of the gym work-out look, this would surely get him the rest.

I have to get her away from him. Was there other way around? Seeing a valet gave me an idea. I might not be able to convince the whole crowd, but a single man is just a snap of fingers away.

The valet shrugged towards Augusto on my command and spoke to him, "Sir, can you please follow me to the parking lot? I can't seem to stop your car alarm from going off."

"Excuse me for a moment!" the Italian businessman quickly mumbled and made his way to the nearest exit.

I let my eyes linger on her for a few moments, trying to *catch and hold onto this moment forever.* Her breathing had eased with his absence, then she got lost in the crowd, saving herself from *the monster* that lays within me.

My hunger was not satisfied with only getting him out of the picture, he had to be gone for good! I followed behind them on the path until we reached a spot that the surveillance cameras didn't catch. "Leave!" I commanded the valet. He followed my words immediately, without having any recollection of what had just happened.

With a little more focus I managed to interrupt the CCTV trans-mission, leaving only grey static dots on their screens. Augusto was now in the middle of the parking lot invisible to them. My fangs were instinctively emerging, not because of hunger, but because of the need for destruction. He had touched something that didn't belong to him and the fine was *death.*

"Good evening, Augusto!" I smirked, feasting on the scared look on his face as soon as he acknowledged my presence.

"D...Damien!" he blabbered. A very unusual thing for a man like him, but they all crack in front of me.

"I told you before not to challenge me again!"

"I-" he didn't get to finish his worthless sentence because my fangs made their way to his neck. His blood had the taste of my revenge and the sweet flavor of hate. These made me drain him completely in just a minute, ripping off his jugular when I finished. He didn't deserve an open casket and I was making sure he wouldn't have one.

The monster inside had to calm down. I got into my car and drove back to my apartment, trying to escape *the increasing need of her.*

~~~

A few moments earlier

Sarah

What the hell was that? I kept asking myself this since the moment I had walked away from him. The stress must be getting to me. Karla's put so much pressure on me arranging this deal that I'm starting to imagine things. He didn't even want to talk to me. Such an arrogant jerk! He didn't let me get two words out before chasing me away. Ahhh...my boss is going to be so pissed.

I'm going to have to close some other deals tonight to try to smooth things over. My manager's position will surely have to wait for a couple of years now. Why couldn't she have just sent someone else on this suicidal mission?

"I can't seem to get away from you. This must be fate!" a seductive voice made its way to my ears. Augusto, the Italian businessman, was standing right next to me, eyes wide open and pointed directly at my cleavage.

I really hate how he thinks that I'll be number 788 or whatever digit he's at on his list.

"I see your business meeting was cut short," he purred rearranging a strand of my hair with one hand and stroking my arm with the other.

I knew where this was going and since my boss has no interest in him, neither do I. I decided to cut this conversation short and spare him the trouble.

"I can say that I pride myself on the art pieces that I've collected over the last couple of years. Over time I have managed to put together a remarkable collection. Since your boss is set on turning this night into a business one, I could offer you a private tour of my house for you to decide if we can work together." He intervened before I had the chance to set things straight.

So many damn words were leaving his mouth in the vain attempt to get me into his bed, when all I wanted to do was to avoid his gaze and admire a little the beauty of this place.

Big crystal chandeliers were hanging from the ceiling providing the room with the much-needed luxury aura, while a big black marble bar was standing in the left corner threatening to disorient more than a few guests during this night.

"What do you say? Can I offer you a drink so you can think my proposal through?" he took me away from studying the surroundings.

I wanted to spit back at him - *there's an open bar you idiot* - but I was interrupted by a valet "Sir, can you please follow me to the parking lot? I can't seem to stop your car alarm from going off."

"Excuse me for a moment!", Augusto quickly mumbled while almost running to the nearest exit.

Ecstatic is just not enough to describe the feeling I was experiencing once he was gone.

Now, I just have to get a hold of Karla and probably serve my sentence. I wouldn't normally be concerned, but she seemed really determined on me landing this deal.

Glitter, sequins, feathers were all shining on designer's dresses, furnishing the saloon with a Hollywood glow. So much money in the same room. I'm more than sure that I could compensate for the price of my failure with only a few closed deals. There she is...

"Karla!"- I spoke to her awkwardly giving her a hint of the outcome.

She crossed her arms and the look she was giving me was certainly not a welcoming one "You're back!?" - she muttered under her breath.

"I... He didn't even want to talk to me. His interest was only on spending the night alongside his date," I rolled my eyes trying to reconfirm her that there was no room for intervention.

Her bottom lip twisted in annoyance and anyone looking on could easily tell that she was about to explode.

"You're fired!!!"

Sculpting my destiny

I spat back at her, "You can't do that! I have worked far too hard for you to do this to me." I was determined to work something out. I didn't lose a year and a half out of my life just so that she could fire me now.

"Not hard enough since you can't get me what I want!" she raised an eyebrow while questioning my professional abilities.

"This is about one single person who happened to be *indisposed* at the time I approached him. Are you judging my value to your company on just this one man?"

"You don't understand... I want the top! Top customers, top collaborators and undoubtedly top agents. If you want to be on top there's no room for mistakes!"

"No one could land him. He's the most antisocial person I ever met! He literally told me to leave the second I opened my mouth, and besides, there's something weird about him."

"Weird, antisocial... I don't care... You blew it. Who knows when I'll have access to an event like this again? I've been chasing this guy for a few years, and I hoped you'd be ready when the time comes."

"You mean to say that you only hired me so I could get Damien?" My blood was reaching boiling point already. I was starting to get the feeling that every single vein in my head was about to explode.

"This is NY! Didn't you find it weird that you got a job at a company like mine the minute you graduated? Your History Art teacher back at the University is a dear friend of mine and knowing about my ambition, she recommended you."

"But why? Why him? Why me?" I shrugged, still unsure about the main reason why she picked me and why did the world end at Damien Arion.

"An old employee of mine managed to stumble upon one of his estates. It was back in Italy, while she was looking for one of her friends that went MIA. Let's just say she wasn't just impressed, she was shocked! This isn't just about the Shang Dynasty vase...he's like an Indiana fucking Jones!"

Her face was turning bright red while her hands started to gesticulate in the air, drawing attention to us. "I don't know where he gets the pieces of art from. Maybe he inherited them, maybe he bought them in illegal auctions. I don't care! I just want in!"

I managed to whisper "Karla..." in order to make her aware that by now we had attracted a great deal of attention.

She quickly stopped her passionate speech and managed to regain her composure. As if she hadn't been screaming at me just a second ago she managed to say quite quietly "Let's step outside!"- she made room between people and headed towards the terrace.

At this point I wasn't even sure if I should be mad, confused, or grateful since this job opportunity was indeed much more than any history art majors usually get.

"Can I ask... Why didn't your former employee try to close a business deal with Mr. Arion?"

Karla's lips corners formed into a smile like I was asking a very childish question. "She tried...all my employees have tried. That's why I hired you. Because everyone else has failed and I believed that you would succeed!"

"Damien is so rarely seen at public events and the ones he does participate at are usually very exclusive and very restricted."

"The only thing that gets his full attention now are beautiful women. Even though I have several female employees, none of them were pretty enough to get a second look from him. I just thought that if someone more *presentable* was to approach him, he may get a little relaxed and open up for negotiations."

I crossed my arms, my eyes gave her dagger like looks as I calmly and coldly asked her "So, you only hired me for my looks?"

"I needed someone that had knowledge in the art field and looked good at the same time... You were my last resort."

"Wow...so, a man I know nothing about is *sculpting my destiny.*" By this time, I was seriously concerned about the impact any of this would have on me and any future jobs I might get offered at any other NY gallery.

"You're actually doing great at work. You have made significant progress over the last year and a half, but you'll still need to prove yourself in order to make me add another zero in your salary."

... Wait ...what? ... I've still got my job?

"I'm confused... Am I fired or am I not?" I needed to get a straight answer from her since this whole '***deal went bad***' attitude was confusing enough.

"You may still be useful," she blurted out placing a hand on her chin like she was conceiving a master plan.

She seemed to have withdrawn into some kind of distant parallel world for a few moments, but quickly snapped out it and muttered "Go get me some clients, we have to make up for the losses. You can forget all about that promotion for now anyway!"

"Ok, Karla," and I was gone before she could change her mind, or come up with some other crazy idea of seducing someone else into working with us.

People may think I'm insane for putting up with her moods, but if I want to attain my goals I have no choice. This has always been my dream and losing this job could easily mean an end to everything I wished for. Also, let's face it, not having to check my wallet every time I go shopping is also a major plus. Even though I am just an assistant, the salary is more than decent and the benefits of having this Gallery on my resume will also be a huge bonus.

I'm determined to close some deals tonight, and although Augusto might be an easy target, I'm not willing to sleep with someone for a contract. A harmless flirt is one thing, but actually sharing a bed with the guy is a whole different game.

I usually have no high morals regarding businesses. I live in NY and I know that sometimes in order to make it big, you have to get into the lion's cage. I don't fear that. I'm actually well capable of deceit, lies and pretty much everything else to get what I want... except for the intimacy part. I can sell you my words, my smiles, my fake promises, but never my feelings or my body.

With Augusto off the client's list, I headed towards a familiar presence, Mrs. Ullmann. I had seen her before at an event I organized back at the gallery and if I recall well enough also in some art magazines. She is an old baroness, the last of her kind in these parts, and of course, she owns an impressive art collection. Not many expensive pieces, unfortunately, as she had had to sell the most valuable ones to support her husband's company. However, there was enough of value remaining to make her one of my interests for the night.

"Good evening, I don't mean to disturb you," I said to the white-haired lady now standing to my left. You could tell she was a beautiful woman back in her youth. Her perfect features were still there, even though she was in her mid-seventies. Time had surely been more than kind to this woman. If I didn't know a little about her bio, I could easily think that she is no older than mid-fifties.

I examined her for a second as her presence was just overwhelming. She had chosen to wear a beautiful handmade silk dress with thousands of little beads sewn in different patterns. You could easily see that it had been made especially for her by a master tailor back when people respected quality and hard work, not just a brand label.

I had loved this lady since the moment I approached her. She was just meandering through time, sending me back into a century-long forgotten. It was just like magic was floating all around her and the kindness of her soul was transcending into my psyche.

"Art" she smiled clinking her champagne glass against mine.

"I'll drink to that every day of the week," Mrs. Ullmann chuckle emanating benevolence.

For the first time, I was actually ashamed of wanting to gain something by approaching her. "Am I that obvious?" I murmured. Her smile was still there and her eyes were captivating me. If I didn't know any better, I would say that they were changing color from brown to light green.

"We've met before, at the gallery. I could never forget someone like you."

"Like me?!" I asked a little confused since my role there had not been that important. I'm certain that the person who gave you a flyer and checked on the staff is more than easily forgotten or passed by, without further thought.

Mrs. Ullmann immediately shook her head, as she said "An art lover such as yourself? You rarely see people like you around." Her smile was telling me something that I didn't completely buy into.

"Would you like to set up an appointment to discuss our mutual interests? I'm sorry for rushing, but my car just came to pick me up," she asked quietly whilst looking at her phone.

"I'd be delighted!" I almost exclaimed with genuine joy. Not only would I be very likely close a deal, but I'll also get to spend some time with this lady. I have this strong feeling that I could learn so much from her. Maybe perfect my manners that had been lost in the metamorphosis of time, or tricks that can help me polish up my taste in art. I didn't know what mysteries she was hiding, but I sure wanted to explore them and learn from them.

"Call me so that we can set something up." She handed me an elegant black business card. I didn't expect anything the less from her.

"I sure will!"

"Have a nice evening," I chuckled, overjoyed not just by the potential deal, but the great opportunity that had presented me with such ease.

"*Sweet dreams, darling*," she responded warmly, making me almost drop my champagne glass.

There's no doubt that tonight was the weirdest evening of my life! On top of all that, I must be hearing things. I have to get my focus back and continue with what I had planned to do so that I can finally get home.

The rest of the evening was spent talking to different people, trying to get them interested in our gallery. Some were, while the rest were much more interested in my cleavage. *Damn, Lala!!!* With a few promises and a lot more disappointments I went home, exhausted, but also intrigued by this night.

One thing kept bothering me though... *I wasn't quite ready to let Damien ruin this chance for me.*

His

Finally, home! I said to myself, closing the apartment door behind me.

This greatly anticipated evening had turned out to be a complete catastrophe that had managed to drain me of all my remaining energy. I just don't want to think about work for a moment longer. It's bad enough that I had spent all Saturday night trying to charm my way into some sleazeball's pockets but I had had to shred a little bit of my self-esteem in the process.

At this point, I didn't care about the dress I was wearing or the designer's shoes... I just wanted to switch off from this world and sleep. The shoes and gown were quickly tossed away into a corner of the room as I headed straight to the shower. Hot water was now crashing all over my body, drop by drop washing the frustrations of the evening's events away. *This feels so perfect* - I closed my eyes allowing all my senses to relax while a love song that I must have picked up during the party played away to me at the back of my mind.

I was moving my head to the rhythm of my thoughts when I felt a pair of lips colliding softly on the soft warm flesh on my shoulders and then gently trailing kisses down my back. I instantly turn, but no one was there to be seen, except that there was a hint of that manly cologne in the air that drunkenly played madness with my senses every night.

It's official! I've lost it!

Between my nocturnal fling and the stress at work, I had managed to *lose my mind.*

Just fucking great!!!

I rinse the rest of the remaining lather off my body, then dry myself and slip into the large cotton t-shirt I usually sleep in.

Finally, I glide between the cool silk sheets, feeding my spirit with the sensations of home. I toss and turn a little since the night's events kept playing on my mind. But soon, as my eyes closed a feeling of peace took control. I couldn't have drifted off for more than a couple of minutes before a hand gently touches my face and a man's body is making room in the sheets behind me.

I know it's **him** as all my senses betray me. I was now entirely his prisoner without a single word having left his lips. I take a deep breath as his torso reached mine, he closes the gap between us to the point where not even molecules of air could flow past our joined bodies.

A lump formed in my throat as the feeling of his lips roaming the side of my neck combined with one of his hands slowly lifting my t-shirt whilst pulling me even closer to him.

I push myself back a little, causing a long soft growl to leave his lips as his trail of kisses reached my soft warm sensitive earlobes.

"Close your eyes," he whispered quietly and even though I had no intention of listening to him, my eyelids instinctively followed his order, ignoring my existence completely.

He then turned me around to face him. As much as I wanted to open my eyes, they remained closed, it was as if there was an invisible scarf covering my them.

I could feel his sweet breath on my lips and soon his tongue was searching for them, commanding them to part as I was willingly pulled into a lustful kiss. His tongue danced against mine with the hunger of a predator tasting its prey and even though it might just be true, I couldn't stop myself. The urge to spend even a few moments with the man of my dreams was just too intense.

There was something between us. *A bond that surpassed all eternity.* The feeling that we shared a connection from previous lifetimes was growing along with the intensity of our kiss.

Small moans escaped from my mouth whilst his hands were lifting my t-shirt with an agonizingly slow rhythm. I could hear him groan as his tongue moved rhythmically against mine, but I knew he was soon going to break our kiss to explore new areas of my skin.

My hands instinctively tangled themselves in his hair as he moved the trail of kisses to my neck, finding the spot that makes my thighs press firmly together in an attempt to extinguish some of the fire that started burning throughout my lower body.

I desperately tried a few times to open my eyes, but it was useless. My desire to see my mystery man had to wait yet again, but at least I can feel his touch a million times more amplified.

He ripped me away from my thoughts as he finally released my aching body from the confines of my t-shirt, leaving me naked before him to admire. I started to tremble in excitement, completely unaware of his next move. I started to wonder... if this is my reaction when he doesn't even touch me, what the hell will I feel when he actually does?

"Te astept de asa mult timp" (*I've been waiting for so long*) he whispered, slowly descending to my chest while all my other senses were dancing in ecstasy.

"I want to see you," I whimpered, begging for this devil to give me at least this one thing, since the wait for him to claim me was making me feel as if I were in Purgatory.

"Patience, my love," he growled, as he captured one of my full aching tips between his lips, rolling his tongue over it. My breath grew short from the pleasure that was now racing through me, taking full control of my body.

He growled hard, slowly grazing my breasts with his teeth, letting his hands travel freely over the rest of my skin, finding new areas to explore every second. *My being* was his... It had been so since *many lifetimes ago*, like a well-remembered connection responding eagerly to his every single touch.

All a sudden I could feel him changing his position, causing my thighs to slowly part, allowing him to place himself between them.

I immediately reacted, forcing my hips down into the bed, preparing for what's to come.

Without any warning he returned to my lips, but this time the kiss was different, more eager, anxious like time was all of a sudden running out on us. I responded in seconds, making my tongue dance around his in my desperate exploration of his mouth.

My pulsating core was now firmly pressed against his hardness, with only a thin piece of material separating us from being as one. As my hips started to arch and gyrate in a slow hypnotic rhythm, he began devouring my skin more eagerly, sucking and nibbling on the side of my neck, then traveling to my chest and repeating the same actions that had already made me almost delirious with pleasure.

The room echoed with the sounds of our desire. The noise made by his trousers buckle coming undone made my heart almost explode out of my chest. I knew that this had released himself from having been imprisoned within since his eagerness was now pressing impressionably against my inner thigh.

Silence suddenly set upon us as my shallow breathing *betrayed* my anticipation in the worse way possible.

Sensing my excitement, but also my awkwardness, his lips crashed upon mine setting a slower, more relaxed pace, pushing back some of my emotions.

One of his hands played with my hair, wrapping it around his fingers, giving me a sensation of contentment, but also making it impossible for me to move. I wished so hard to open my eyes, but they were still not in my control. My desire to do so only increased with the feeling of his tip moving against my folds.

His grinding around my inner thigh was leaving me powerless. The control this man had over my very being was truly unbelievable.

I am without question *made to be his as he is made to be mine.* Only one movement separates us now from pure ecstasy as a small pressure was building up against me which was making me fully aware that the time was **now**. *This was it! The perfect-*

Beep, beep, beep!!!

No!

What's happening!?

I screamed as I jumped naked out of bed searching the room for answers.

No, no, no!!!

This can't be possible!!! I muttered as I closed the curtains against the rising sun, then jumping back into bed and covering myself with all the sheets I could find.

Sleep!!! I begged myself, desperate to continue where I'd left off.

Goddammit!!! Just sleep!!! I ordered myself again and again, this time pressing my pillow over my face in an effort to take away the light. I realized that I had more chance of committing suicide by smothering myself with this than actually falling asleep.

Since I usually am a fighter, not a quitter, I rolled in bed for a few more hours trying to catch the mystery man again... but of course and to my despair, with no success. I even tried bed yoga which, although I consider it a little bit boring, wasn't enough to put me back to sleep.

When I finally decided to give up it was already noon. So, with the battle lost, I got out of bed, cursing my way to the kitchen. On my way there I grabbed the robe that I had thrown the day earlier onto the living room couch.

Now that I come to think about it, *I distinctly remember putting a t-shirt on last night when I got to bed.*

I really hope that I'm not losing my mind because I don't intend spending my salary on shrinks. Besides, at what those people charge I'm pretty sure that I couldn't afford the rent for my apartment and living on their couch doesn't seem to be an option.

Snapping my neck, I pressed the magic button that would start to prepare me my morning poison and soon my favorite mug was filled with the awakening liquor. I sat down at the kitchen table and saw the black business card Mrs. Ullmann handed me last night.

That's another thing I didn't remember doing.... taking the piece of paper out of the bag and placing it on the table. I really hope this isn't a young age form of Alzheimer's. But, by now I have serious thoughts that maybe I should get checked. I rubbed my eyes to clear away some of my morning fog... The same two orbs that betrayed me last night... But that was just a dream. *Right*?

Finally, pulling myself together I decided to dial the number on the business card.

"Hello, Sarah... I was expecting your call!" her voice answered on the other end before I could even make a sound.

But how did she know who it was?!

Home

A cold shiver ran across my body as the surprise or Mrs. Ullmann recognizing me without actually getting to say a single word was a little overwhelming.

"How did you know who I was?" I finally asked her but not before trying to swallow the knot that formed in my throat.

"No one ever calls me these days my dear," she answered with a very relaxed voice. My mind was beginning me to believe her.

"I... I called you to set an appointment for this week."

"I have to leave for Paris tomorrow and I won't be back for a month. But you can come over now if you wish. I do have a few paintings that I want to sell. *Come! I'll be waiting!*"

"I'll get dressed and be right there."

"That would be lovely! You have the address on the business card! See you here soon, my dear!"

An overwhelming sense of joy took control of me as a feeling of family was settling in. It was like I was going to visit some long-lost relative.

I quickly looked around my dressing room. Even though Sundays were normally my '*casual jeans day*', I chose a more stylish outfit for this visit. I wore an over the knee tight white skirt with a light nude blouse and the right pair of heels. Perfect!

I run out the door, anxious to take a look into Mrs. Ullmann's past.

As I waited for the cab to arrive, I couldn't help noticing that the feel of fall was approaching. The faded smell of cold air along with the yellowish color of the leaves was bringing a certain melancholy into my heart. Like I just found a long forgotten path that I'll eventually have to follow in order to reach **home**.

A cab pulled up sharply beside me *"Hey, I'm on the clock here lady!"* the cab driver was screaming through his window while honking.

You have to love NY! Where else can you find this many rude people in one single place?

As I got inside the cab you couldn't help but notice the 20's tunes that were playing on the radio. If you closed your eyes, one could almost swear there was an old gramophone sitting next to you. Its needle playing in the groove of an old vinyl record, extracting the all too familiar crackling sound that my ears feasted upon.

I know that I'm different. Various things from the past bring me such joy, but also sadness. It's like I was supposed to have been born in a different century, and how I missed it all. It's not only art... Sometimes I even find this feeling while reading an old worn paperback book or visiting an old building.

I always craved for something more, for a world that couldn't really exist... *I always craved for him. The man that visits me in my dreams every night, leaving me empty without his presence every morning.*

"$18.95", the cab driver spat out at me the second we pulled in front of the building identified from the black classy business card. I quickly paid him, happy to get out of his cab. As much as I liked his taste in music, I loathed the thick stale smell of old cigarettes and gasoline that was impregnated in the car upholstery.

The penthouse, of course. Where else would the rich and famous live? Well, in this case, the not so rich, but apparently still wealthy enough to afford the top floor of this impressive building. The doorman showed me the elevator I needed to take in order to reach my destination. The doors opened letting me into a luxurious box waiting patiently to carry me up to the penthouse suite, my destination.

As the metal doors slid open the view presented to me was stunning. I stepped out into a large Victorian style room, its walls a sea of art. A truly *magical* place.

I literally didn't know where to look first. Who would have thought that a NY penthouse could look like this? The grace of an era long forgotten still lingered in this room and a soft cedar smell invaded all senses.

"Right on time!" Mrs. Ullmann made her way in from a small hallway just across the room.

"Come, my dear. Let me introduce you to my prized possession," she smiled gliding down the corridor she came from.

It gets better than this!? I asked myself following her until I reached a smaller room which wasn't any less impressive. It was laid out like a small museum, with a few central pieces well placed on glass pedestals.

"Egyptian" Mrs. Ullmann said whilst looking at a golden cat statue that was covered in hieroglyphs "It's supposed to be magic... The statue. But what's its worth; if I don't know how to read the writings on it? No one does... I have shown it to several archeologists, but they couldn't decipher it."

"Magic?!" I could hardly contain myself from laughing, slightly convinced that this woman could be a little insane.

"In Egyptian culture cats are supposed to protect you from evil spirits. I believe that the hieroglyphs carved on the figure are the words you're supposed to chant in order for it to protect you".

Yup... Definitely a little lunatic.

"You could have chosen *the casual jeans*; I wouldn't have minded. I do appreciate class and elegance but above all else, I love the liberty of just being yourself." As Mrs. Ullmann spoke these words, I felt that my legs were about to fail me. This couldn't be all coincidences. The fact that she remembered me... she knew who it was on the phone, without me getting a chance to say something. And now this... How did she know about the jeans? Have I told her? Am I losing my mind? I'm starting to feel like I'm hallucinating.

At this point, I wasn't sure if I should even trust myself to speak to her... Maybe I'm crazy... It must be from stress! Definitely! I've often heard of people that imagined seeing things due to fatigue.

"Dear, are you feeling all right? I'll go get you a cup of tea. Lay down on the sofa until I come back," she took my hand guiding me to the divan that sat in a corner of the room.

I must look just like a wacko. What normal person comes to your house and almost has a seizure? This is it! Doctors appointment first thing tomorrow morning. Maybe I can still get help.

"Here you go!" Mrs. Ullmann handed me a cup of tea with a genuine smile plastered on her face, while my mind was still in turmoil.

"See that empty spot on the right? There used to hang a Monet. My husband and his business made me give it up... Love is a very complicated feeling. But what worth do material things have when the souls are connected?" She smiled again with a certain melancholy in her look.

I took a few seconds outs to analyze the room a little better. It felt just like I've stepped into a different era. Even though the valuable pieces were gone I couldn't complain about the quality of the remaining ones.

Firstly, I examined the central pieces. A Greek bronze vase, probably dated a few hundred years BC proudly sitting next to the Egyptian cat and a baroque gold hand-made cup, with fine jewels embedded on the sides shining through the glass that surrounded it.

The paintings in the room were also very well selected. Excellent taste was certainly a quality Mrs. Ullmann didn't lack. Most of them were from the Renaissance period, but there was one that didn't quite fit in. The one that caught my eye was the representation of a long dark corridor with only dim lights revealing parts of the walls. Some might say a creepy mysterious place... But for me, it felt like *home?*

"It attracts you, doesn't it?... **The darkness,**" she said looking at me while my heart actually stopped for a second.

"It's in you... You can't escape it. *I wished there was a way you could,* but it's *like a magnet, reaching out to its other half.*"

Mrs. Ullmann placed her cup of tea on a small wooden Victorian table that was next to the couch "You must think I'm some crazy old woman... Maybe I am, who knows?"

I swallowed hard, a knot forming in my throat as I gathered myself to formulate a coherent sentence "Can we please discuss what I came here for?".

"I'm sorry my dear. You're right. I sometimes tend to talk a little too much," she said in a voice tinged with sadness. "I've called you here because I'd like to sell a few more paintings. This will be the last sacrifice I'm willing to make in order to get the company back on its feet. I feel like I'm giving away my babies."

Mrs. Ullmann spoke with such sadness that I felt my eyes getting wetter. What we do for love. "Don't worry, I'll make sure you get the best for them... Even if my boss would kill me." I smiled, determined to do so. I can easily assess their worth, and getting her a more than fair price wouldn't be that hard.

"Thank you! I know you will! Come, let me take you to the pieces I wish to sell."

"They're not in here?" I inquired, curious to see the paintings as soon as possible.

"I'm not selling another piece from this room! You actually passed by them on your way in. They're in the living room."

I stood up and we headed toward the door.

"I think I saw something, but you have so many beautiful pieces that I didn't even know where to look."

"It's ok, dear. Take your time. I was hoping that you would have a few free hours for us to discuss this a little more."

"Sure! I have the whole day off!" I giggled excitedly; this magnificent woman actually wants to spend her time with me.

"These would be the ones I'm willing to part from," Mrs. Ullmann said as soon as we reached the living room. She shifted her gaze towards the south wall where five fine paintings hung.

Just like the paintings in the little showroom, these ones were also from the Renaissance period, not as valuable, but put together I think they would bring a five zeros total. "Not so exciting as the *young* man the other night." Mrs. Ullmann smiled, making a cold shiver traveling my body.

What the Hell is going on here?

My curse

I took a deep breath, overwhelmed and exhausted at the same time from all the knowledge this woman had. But one thing I'm sure of, this is happening, she's saying these things to me and I'm not crazy. I can't be!

The sweet smile spread further on her face "*Damien*; I'm referring to him in case you're confused as to who I was talking about."

I couldn't put a sentence together and once more my thoughts were bouncing between reality and fantasy. Nothing made sense anymore.

"He's charming, everything about him is meant to allure you...The deadliest always are like this." She took a deep breath and continued her thoughts "I wish I could tell you to run my dear, never looking back and that *you would be able to do so*. But I'm far too old to believe such fairy tales. Destiny will always find its way into our lives, controlling them to the smallest detail, because *in the end,* you can never escape your *fate*."

"I don't want to scare you. That's the last thing I have in mind... You're so special, my child... Maybe the last one of your kind."

My lower lip began to tremble, as was the rest of my body. I feared what she was about to say because, in a way, I always felt that I wasn't like ordinary people.

"This world isn't always how we see it to be. Other forces coexist here amongst us. Strong forces that can either be ruled by darkness or light. People called them different names in history... witches, monsters, vampires, sorcerers, demons. Mostly their names were defined by how their human shape manifested itself."

Mrs. Ullmann took a moment of silence then turned her head, looking out the window. "My powers allow me to see the past and predict small pieces of the future, but I can also see a person's true nature."

"And, no... I'm not a witch that makes secret potions out of frogs and snails' eyes. These are just fantasy stories invented by scared people who always distort the truth."

"Are you telling me you have the power to see the past?" I inquired. my voice tinged with doubt, ready to ask her a trick question.

"Sarah..." Mrs. Ullmann giggled... "You broke your leg when you were five, your mother used to make lasagna every Sunday, which you hated, and Zack Summers stole your first kiss in the girl's locker room".

I placed my hand on my abdomen, attempting to push back the lump in my stomach, trying to find a logical explanation on how she could know these things.

"If you want, I can tell you more but I highly doubt that you'd like to relive some of the *interesting* moments of your life here with me".

I shook my head "No... that's enough!" The room was almost spinning and even though this day was the weirdest of my life, I still wanted to learn more "What is so special about me?" I asked a little scared to learn the truth but still convinced that I needed it.

"Your quite unique, my child. Your powers come from the beginning of time but are neither evil nor good. You are the only being that can decide how you want to use them and in what camp you wish to choose," she said giving me another of her benevolent smiles

"I don't understand" shaking, I took a seat on the couch.

"Let see if I can make things a little bit clearer. You are like an amplifier. If you choose to learn magic, you'll be the strongest witch... if you choose the dark side and want to be a demon, you'll be the most powerful one and if you'll turn into a vampire, you'll be the dominant member of the species."

"Vampires..." the letters blurted out, being the sole word that fully drew my attention.

"Yes, *vampires*. The simple word makes the blood run through your veins faster... It's ok... I understand".

"Vampires have actually been around since the beginning of time and bare different names in cultures all around the world. From the ghouls in Arabia to the goddess Sekhmet in Ancient Egypt."

"The first historical mentions of them comes from Mesopotamia. Ancient Greeks and Romans also have legends about bloodsucking demons.

Still, the most known version that practically all modern society knows about vampires appeared in the 18th century. But, for the people that still reside in secluded villages all around the world, they are the living dead or evil spirits that come out at night to claim their tribute. Many villagers still don't go out alone after sunset and close their windows after nightfall with wooden blinds."

"Wait, isn't this just a story Bram Stoker wrote?"

"A story based on truth. They're supposed to originate from a region in Southeastern Europe, called Transylvania, and that's not entirely false. Throughout time most of them migrated to different countries, mainly drawn by blood and power lust. So, between the 13th and 18th century an important concentration of vampires settled there since the region was more than adequate for their living necessities. A secluded area surrounded by mountains and forests, the blood taste of the wars and the mirage of power and wealth. A perfect living habitat... Until someone noticed and the myth became reality.

The unwanted attention made most of them leave, moving on

to other locations where their true identity could be easily kept hidden." Mrs. Ullmann raised an eyebrow like she was trying to elaborate on a devious plan. "You're still undecided if you should believe me or not."

"I don't know what to believe anymore. I'm so confused... Who am I? What am I supposed to be? I've always felt a weird attraction to myths, antique artifacts-"

"And darkness, my child... I know you're attracted to it... It's his calling... **His** soul has been searching for you for ages. But you can still fight it... You can still choose. That's your greatest gift. You've been born as a human and you have the opportunity to choose. Choose to live a normal life or choose the path of light or darkness. But it's *your* decision to make!"

"This sounds more like a *curse* than a gift. Every other person would choose the path of light... But, I can't... I can't choose now."

"You don't have to. No one is forcing you to do so. You'll know when the time is right."

The electrical sound of the elevator's motor warned us of its approach. The doors opened and a very presentable gentleman stepped into the living room.

"Good evening, ladies"- he smiled, walking past me and heading towards Mrs. Ullmann, whose beam was again lightening the whole room.

Her arms came around his neck and she kissed the man just like a schoolgirl and not like a woman in her 80s "Good evening, my love!".

After their short moment of intimacy, her eyes turned on me "I'm sorry dear, my husband and I share a very strong connection. I believe you *know* what I'm talking about." The corner of her lip raised a little even though she made an attempt to hide her smirk.

"I do hope my queen hasn't filled your head with all sort of nonsense. She tends to read too many books and is firmly convinced that most of them are true. I must admit that it's mainly my fault because I do spend much more time working than I should."

"I think I should get going. It's already late"- I stuttered as I went to retrieve my bag.

"I'll go change and then take you out to dinner." Mr. Ullmann kissed his wife's forehead. "Have a nice evening!" He greeted me before entering the long lobby and disappearing from our sight.

"I'll make you an official offer tomorrow and will make sure you'll get a more than fair price for your paintings," I nodded while walking towards the elevator.

"I'm sure of that! I'll send them to the gallery before I leave for Paris. And ...be careful!" her voice whispered right next to my ear. But how had she moved from the opposite corner of the living room to next to me in just a second?

I could hardly contain my breathing, trying to maintain the balance between Mr. Ullmann's words and everything else that happened since I've met this woman.

"*Avoid him at all costs*." Mrs. Ullmann murmured again, drawing my full attention.

"Can I ask who exactly are you talking about?" I inquired even though my soul knew the answer.

"You know who I'm talking about. Damien... *Damien will be your destruction.*"

A hundred explanations came to my mind, about how I have nothing to do with him and our paths will never meet again. But I could formulate only one sentence *"I'll try."*

Mrs. Ullmann grabbed me into a warm embrace, just like I was saying goodbye to a family member. I hugged her back, filling myself with her positive energy.

"If you ever need anything, I'll be here for you," she stated as the elevator door was closing and I was waving goodbye.

I left the building and headed towards home, overwhelmed

by what I just found out. Confusion was still the main issue that dominated my current life. I knew that what she told me couldn't be real, but I felt that it was.

Is she just an old woman who has lost the sense of reality, or does a different reality exist?

The questions that were piling up in my mind barely let me get any sleep. So, my nightly encounter had to wait until tomorrow evening, since by the time I managed to close my eyes, the first ray of light was already kissing the window.

Cornered

I'm going to break that damn alarm clock. I muttered, completely irritated by the electronic sound it was making.

I couldn't have gotten more than two hours of sleep. But bills have to be paid, so skipping work was not an option.

Yesterday's events still lingered in my mind. Even though I wanted to believe that Mrs. Ullmann was just a crazy old woman, deep down inside I knew that this wasn't the case. I got out of bed, took a quick shower, did the rest of my morning routines and went into the dressing room to find something to wear.

New life, new clothes. I said to myself and picked up a black dress that still had the tag on. I was keeping that for some special business meeting, but I decided there's no better time than the present. Besides, having a new piece of clothing always cheers me up... And I definitely needed cheering up these days.

I still had some time left, so I decided to prepare myself a coffee. During the week I usually get my dose from the cafe across the street from work... But since that's my only addiction, one cup is never enough.

As I was enjoying my peace and quiet, the doorbell rang. I had no doubt as to who that was. When the door opened my suspicions were confirmed.

"Why didn't you call me?" Lala asked while entering my apartment.

"Let me guess... You didn't end up having steamy sex on Damien's kitchen floor?"

"You watch too many movies." I rolled my eyes at her, without being able to help myself from fantasizing about a scene like that. Damien's muscular body pinning me to the kitchen tiles with one hand, while ripping my clothes off with the other.

"You're imagining it, aren't you!" Lala chuckles busting my day-dream.

Yup... I'm pathetic. I'm cheating on the imaginary man of my dreams with a daytime fantasy of a man who didn't even want to speak with me for even a moment. *Who needs real life when I have all of this going for me*? I took a large sip of coffee, hoping that it might get me back to the world we actually live in. "I'm not image-"

"Liar!" She started laughing calling me out on my newly de-served name.

"What are you doing here anyway?" I pouted, trying to change the subject.

"I just got off work and wanted to check up on you to see how the gala went?" Lala pulled me into a hug... I hate morning hugs. They seem to suck the air out of me. There aren't many things that I can deal with before noon.

"Tell me straight away! I want to get going," she pulled me closer to her.

I have to get out of this trap!

"Nothing... Nothing happened... He wasn't interested in me!" I kept my distance from her, searching for my coffee cup.

"I tried speaking to him, but he blew me off in less than a minute. He was much more interested with the woman that ac-companied him and I don't blame him. She was stunning."

At some point, I tried even convincing myself that I didn't find him attractive... I guess *Liar* should be my new nickname.

"Did your boss give you a hard time about it?"

"She almost fired me, but I convinced her that she should let me keep my job. I'm trying to get her other deals to compensate." Even though she was my best friend, I couldn't tell her about my newfound abilities, or the lack of them for now. I'm not sure she would be able to deal with my craziness too well.

"Bitch!" Lala muttered, expressing once again her opinion of my boss.

"And nothing else exciting?"

"No, nothing else." I didn't care to mention Augusto so, I won't get her crying about my missed opportunity.

"Ahhh... They should invite me next time. You're such a bore!" Lala chuckled heading towards the door.

"I'll leave you to it. I know you're not a morning person and besides, I'm sleepy."

"You disappoint me! I was hoping that at least you'd have some one-night stand with a prince or a duke you've met over at the party. The best I usually get is some bored waiter... or a bartender if I'm lucky." She shrugged breaking my heart with her bad luck.

I couldn't help myself from laughing. "Get lost!" I've pointed my finger towards the door, letting her know that she is free to leave. The sooner, the better. Tough love, I call it. And even though we're sometimes ironic or sarcastic to one another, we love each other like sisters.

"You still owe me a night out!" she screamed, rushing down the staircase.

And *I* was having doubts about my sanity...

***

I soon left for work, but seeing Karla's face after the weekend wasn't on the top of my favorite list.

Chills started running through my whole body, even though it was very sunny outside. Must be from the fatigue. I ignored the symptoms my body was sending and continued walking until I reached the subway. I hate the crowds, but it's the fastest way to work.

As usual, I bought two coffees. One for me and one for Karla then headed to the gallery door.

One of my colleagues greeted me as I entered, but there was something off. Her look was confused as if she wanted to say more than "Hello," but she managed to contain herself.

Who knows, I might be imagining things. The last couple of days had been rather crazy.

On my way to Karla's office, I took a glimpse at some empty spots on the walls where Mrs. Ullmann's paintings will fit perfectly. I'll deal with that in a bit.

As usual, she was not in. So, I left her coffee on the desk and headed towards my own.

Great! Someone left their junk all over my space! I muttered under my breath grabbing the coat that was left on my chair and what seemed to be a file from the desk counter.

"Who left their stuff on my table?" I growled, visibly irritated. This thing used to happen all the time when I first came here. People would always throw files, even their jackets when in a rush because mine was the closest desk to the door.

"That would be us," Karla responded entering the room accompanied by a woman about my age.

I knew from the moment I saw them that this isn't going to end well, and even though my first instinct was to ask *What the fuck is going on here?* I managed to keep my manners and swallowed my words.

"This is Sapphire," Karla introduced the new girl to me...*Great! A stripper's name."* As you may have guessed this is your new co-worker," my boss devilishly smiled, showing me her perfectly pearl white teeth.

"I didn't know that you were looking for another employee!" I leaned on the desk and supported my arm on the counter. I had a really bad feeling about this and taking a quick peek at the file on my desk, confirmed it.

Damien Arion. His name was written on it, as a reminder of my failure.

It seems that Karla wasted no time in finding a replacement for me. And seeing me as her last chance quickly transformed into try number twenty-something.

I must admit that the girl in front of me was beautiful. Perfect, I might say. Long golden locks framed her small face, adding elegance to her posture. Her pale flawless complexion made her big almond eyes draw even more attention. The whole Miss Ideal look can easily trap any man under her spell.

"I'm thinking about opening a new manager position." Karla spoke crossing her arms like she was making a point.

Does she actually think she can give out the position I've dreamt about ever since I got here, to someone else? And even worse... On her first day in?

"Is this about...?" I paused, unsure if I should continue.

"It's ok. Sapphire knows what she's here for," my boss clarified the situation.

I ground my teeth, pushing back the cursing that was going on in my head. Sure, I could tell her about Mrs. Ullmann's paintings, but I don't think she'd care. Even if she did, I promised a more than fair deal which meant not much room for profit.

"Don't worry, I studied art back in high school. I know all about painters and stuff." Sapphire mentioned, trying to convince me of her *qualifications*.

I wasn't the least impressed, and her credentials didn't involve opening her mouth... At least not for speaking... Karla must be desperate.

"Let me guess...aspiring model?" I asked, receiving an annoyed look from my boss.

"Actress"- she proudly answered, not sensing my irony.

If I had to choose sides right now, I'd definitely choose evil and turn both this dumb doll and my boss into some gargoyles or other repulsing creatures... *Mental institution facility, I'm on my way.*

Was I cornered? ... Probably.... Desperate? .... Definitely! So, in those few moments I made a decision. Mr. Arion is not going to stand in the way of my career... neither some *"aspiring actress\"* that Karla considers to have enough plastic surgeries to seduce her way into his life.

In a moment of madness, the first second they weren't looking I threw the file in my bag. "I have to go! I have to close a deal... Someone who I met at the party," I blabbered heading towards the door.

"Just not the right person." Karla needed to point out the obvious.

I turned around and gave her a faded smile "Yes... Just not the right person."

Seconds later I was on the sidewalk trying to collect my thoughts and figure out what I have to do. There wasn't much mystery about that since there was only one road from now on.

Dismissing all Mrs. Ullmann has told me, all the warnings she had given me. *Here I am, less than 24 hours later, prepared to enter Damien's world.*

.

Food?

My hands were shaking as I went through Damien's file. Apparently, he lives in a building on 10th Avenue. That's not that far from here, but I should still grab a cab to get there.

I waved my hand for more than 5 minutes, trying to get one of the yellow cars to stop and just as I decided to take another form of transport A cab pulled in right beside me and the driver signaled me to hop in. The first break I caught today.

I gave him the address then closed my eyes for a second, asking myself what exactly was I doing. But when I want something, there's no chance in the world I won't get it. An internal turmoil gets control of me every time and I can't find peace until things turn out the way I want. It's not something that I force myself to do. It's just that's the way I have always been.

Maybe a control freak, maybe a fighter... but *always a winner.* That's why I'm having so much trouble giving up this job and accepting my failure.

Today, I'm holding all the cards and I will turn my defeat into a success. I don't plan on seducing my way in this time. I'll just play the determination card and I won't take no for an answer.

My inner motivational speech was working and once the car pulled to a stop, I got out, raised my eyes up and admired the building.

An impressive skyscraper that was made almost entirely of glass was standing tall, defying all other constructions around it. This is the right place since the address from the entrance corresponded with the one on the file.

"Hey! My money!" the cab driver shouted after me and I realized that I was walking away from the car without paying.

"Sorry! Here you go!" I quickly took the money out of my wallet and handed it over to the driver.

"Tourists"- he muttered and drove off in a rush, making me laugh at his statement.

The imposing building caught my attention again. Like I was watching the outside world for the last time, I took a quick look around me while my steps were leading me to the entrance door.

The floor and the walls were made from big tiles of black marble with small golden flakes. Even though I've seen some luxury buildings before in my line of work, this one surpassed them all.

"Good morning!" the security guard at the reception greeted me, making me realize that it was only 10 am.

I hope Damien didn't get to bed too late last night.

"Where to, Miss?" the guard asked me.

"To Mr. Arion's penthouse," I answered very convincingly, as if I had been there a hundred times before.

"Mr. Arion doesn't live in the penthouse. Can you give me your name to check if you're on his visiting list?"

"My name is Sarah Edison, but this is a last-minute appointment. I don't think that he had time to put it on your list," I doubtfully looked at the security guard, trying to intimidate him.

"She must be one of his *friends.* You know that he never tells us anything," another security guard approached the one that had just interrogated me.

"Just let her pass... I need this job and you know how he gets," he continued, winking at me.

"The minus one floor... That's where Mr. Arion is living"- the guard muttered getting from behind his desk and walking me to the elevator.

Minus one... Does he mean the basement? Why would someone that rich live underground, and not a couple of hundred feet above? After all, the higher you live in this town the greater your social status.

Reaching its level, the elevator doors opened, but to my surprise, I wasn't in some hi-end designer's living room.

I found myself standing in a small hallway and in front of me there was a massive metal door.

The sound of the elevator doors closing behind me as the security guard was returning to his desk made me almost jump, unable to control my anxiety any longer.

I tried controlling my emotions and approached the door, looking for a doorbell or another way to announce my presence. I couldn't find any, so I decided to knock, which released a vibrant metallic sound that ran through every single bone in my body.

Waiting for the door to open I felt cold air filling the room. But, at the same time an all too familiar warmth that made me want to cuddle in my bed and close my eyes so that I can be reunited with my mysterious unknown man I long for.

A dim light filled the hallway as the door parted and a woman emerged from behind it.

She was around 50, but you could see that life hasn't been easy for her. Even though she had an elegant white shirt, by the looks of her hands I believed that she was an employee and not family.

"Can I help you?" she asked positioning herself right in front of me just as I was going to enter without asking permission.

"Hello! I'm here to see Mr. Arion," I answered with all confidence that I could gather at that moment.

"Is he expecting you?" she asked, but this time, stepping away from the door frame as she was letting me in.

"I don't think so, but I won't keep him long." I crossed my arms while peering straight into her eyes.

She looked at me with doubt but signaled me to head in. I wasn't going to wait for her to tell me twice, so I took a few steps until I reached the most breathtaking room, I ever set eyes on.

The new gothic style was definitely the main focus of the room's design. A few luxurious chandeliers were hanging imposingly from the ceiling while black wallpaper with Victorian patterns decorated the walls.

The light was dim and some might even say that it emanated a creepy atmosphere. For me, it brought peace like I just found my stream of relaxation.

My greedy eyes scanned quickly across the space as from the second I stepped into the room I couldn't help but notice the plentitude of art pieces and artifacts. In a way, I was eager to see them all but I was even more eager to see *him*.

My boss was right. He is a modern Indiana Jones as he seems to discover a great amount of very valuable art pieces. Some of them were even thought to be forever lost in the depths of time.

I could stay right here in this room for a few centuries without even getting tired of admiring these wonders. I must admit that the man that owns them is becoming, with each one of my heartbeats, more alluring to me.

"*Food*?" the woman who let me in asked while her eyes were examining me from head to toe.

"No thank you, I'm not hungry!" I politely answered just to arouse considerable laughter out of her.

"Please wait here! I'll let him know about your presence," the woman said, still giggling, then headed towards a door at the end of the room.

I didn't think about her too much as a painting grabbed my full attention.

The art piece portrayed a man in his mid-twenties. The most beautiful green piercing eyes and night-black hair were the features that mesmerized me on the spot. There was something very odd about this particular painting. The man in it was definitely Damien, but that couldn't be possible because the picture was at least three hundred years old.

I took a deep breath and tried to convince myself that it was probably a relative of his from the past. I'm possibly overreacting again and see things where they're not. But this time it didn't work, because there was one detail that didn't let me calm my nerves.

Even though, let's presume, that there's the slightest chance that another man could look just like him, the tattoo on his neck gave him away.

It was Damien! In a 300 years old painting!

But how is this possible? Maybe I'm mistaken and my art knowledge is failing me just now. This is the only logical explanation that I can think of.

The visit at Mrs. Ullmann's penthouse started repeating in my mind and her stories did not seem like fairy tales anymore.

I have to take a closer look. Maybe this painting is just made with modern techniques so that it would look old. There are indeed some methods to do that, the same ones that painter's use to falsify art pieces. When I was first hired at the gallery, I took some classes to be able to tell genuine paintings apart from forgeries.

I took a few steps closer and started studying it harder. Sure, it would have been much nicer to be able to take it down, but I don't think that taking someone else's painting off the wall fits in the good manners code.

A cracking sound reached my ears as the door which the women had gone through earlier was slowly opening.

My heart skipped several beats and I started thinking that it could entirely stop from the weird excitement that was affecting my usually contained posture.

"Mr. Arion is tired and asked you to wait for him until he has rested," the woman spoke after entering the room.

Yes, I was for some unknown reason excited by the idea of seeing him. The fact that he didn't send her to kick me out gave me hope.

"I will show you to your room," the woman said and immediately turned around to go back through the door.

"My room?!" I sheepishly asked while following her.

"The room you'll have to wait in until Damien is rested. I suggest that you do the same," she said as we entered a hallway that made me gasp silently inside. It was all too familiar; I had seen this place before. It was the same one that was in Mrs. Ullmann's painting. The same dark long corridor that brought me the comforting feeling of home.

Was I home?

The guest room

The woman closed the door behind her, leaving me alone in the *"guest room."*

As the apartment was underground. It had no windows or any other contact with the outside world. The room was gently lit by subtle levels of low light that were giving a deepening feeling of mystery and isolation.

There were only a few pieces of furniture in the room. They consisted of a large bed covered in dark grey holstering, a small black wooden table, a TV and a few bookshelves.

Since I'm not really a TV fan I couldn't be bothered to search for the remote control. I decided instead to grab a book to help pass my time until Damien finishes resting.

While I was looking through the book titles, I distinctly heard the sound of heels walking past my door. I couldn't distinguish if they were heading in the direction I had come from or going further down the corridor. The one thing I knew for sure was that it wasn't the woman who had let me in. Her shoes had much smaller and thicker heels than the ones I just heard which were much higher and thinner, similar to the ones I usually wear.

A feeling of discomfort started to take hold of me as I realized that he's probably making me wait because he's tired from a long night between another woman's legs. This shouldn't be my concern. I needed to focus my attention on my mission, getting him to accept the collaboration with our gallery.

I turned my eyes back to the bookshelf. *Ulysses* by James Joyce was the title that caught my attention. The fact that it was called *pornography* at the time it was published made me chuckle since the meaning of this term is so different these days. I picked up the book and felt it's fine leather covers. This was an expensive edition, probably limited. I was more than happy to be able to enjoy it. I got on the bed, took off my shoes and opened the precious manuscript to feast my eyes on the words within.

Before I had turned over a couple of pages, I fell asleep, letting the book slip from my hand. The bed was so comfortable and the sheets so soft that my body quickly found the perfect sleeping position and was all set to make up for all my lost nights.

All of a sudden, a hand tangled itself in my hair keeping my head in place so that I won't be able to move. I knew who it was, but this time *'the man from my dreams'* was different, much hungrier than before.

I stood still waiting for his next move, hearing only the beating of my pounding heart and from time to time my shallow breath trembling while leaving my chest.

"Close them," his demanding voice growled on my neck. My eyes were no longer following my commands, but his.

He positioned himself between my thighs, raising my dress to allow me to wrap my legs around his waist. His *lust* for me was now pressing on my aching core. I didn't know which to be shocked about, the speed in which this all was happening or the fact that he was so *eager* in just a few seconds after his first touch.

His body leaned over me so that his lips could find mine and start a passionate kiss. His tongue pushed them to part without asking permission and started exploring my mouth with such intensity that the mere pulses of his flesh against mine were making me wet in expectation.

I gasped as he cupped a breast and massaged it through the material of the dress. But soon, he let out a long growl of annoyance and lifted me up on his waist so he could gain access to the zipper of my dress. The second my clothing was released he pulled it off and threw the light material across the room, gripping my body even closer to his.

I wrapped my arms around his neck, but he pulled them away, laying me on my back and pinning my limbs above my head.

"Don't move!" he ordered. My arms listened, making me a *puppet in his hands*.

His sweet mouth started traveling my chest, pulling my bra down and grazing my quivering tips with his teeth, until they hardened from the pleasure.

I wanted to move, but the way his invisible power was taking control of me only intensified all of my senses. The domination he asserted over my body was making me his unclaimed slave.

I was getting greedy to feed on the feeling of all of my skin being roamed by his tongue. My hips fastened on his waist and started slowly rotating, grinding on his arousal, trying to feel him as close I can before we run out of time again. He let out another groan and left my chest so that he would again explore my neck.

His tongue was the first to touch my collarbone, but soon I felt a much sharper object traveling across my body. Initially, I thought it may be his teeth, yet it was too pointed to be that.

I started getting a little nervous, especially not being able to see what was happening. But, as one of his hands made its way between my thighs ripping my panties and throwing them next to my dress, all of my rational thinking was gone.

Long grinding movements were making me push myself harder into the mattress in my desperate attempt to control what was happening to me, and hopefully keep a little of my sanity.

His kisses turned into slow nibbles on my skin while his hand was descending down on my sensitive area, right between my satin flesh.

My whole body trembled at his contact and the rhythm his fingers acquired was spreading electric shocks throughout my body.

After descending from my neckline, his tongue swirled for a few moments on my nipples, as they ached with the need for his attention. Then he pushed my legs further apart so that his torso could slip in-between them.

His kisses started moving downwards. I could barely contain my excitement as I knew exactly where this was going. The warmth of his mouth on my sensitive skin made me melt instantly and once his tongue started applying pressure on my clit, I was a goner.

I tried thinking of something else so that I could at least last a minute, but he was the main thing on my mind right now.

One of his fingers started slowly grinding inside while his tongue was massaging my folds. Then it started to curl, reaching a spot that made me almost jump from the bed. He held me in position and seeing my reaction he slipped another finger inside, filling me up completely.

If Paradise exists, this should be the main activity there.

My moans were uncontrollable at this point. The pace of his fingers was catching up to the one that his tongue had set while moving against my swollen nub. My toes were curling with every action of his and all I could think about was how bad I want to feel him fully claiming me.

Soon, I couldn't contain myself anymore and an explosion of pleasure filled my body, making it spasm under his every touch.

"Damien," I whimpered as the waves of ecstasy were still traveling my body, **without realizing the mistake**... *If it was a mistake.*

In a glimpse he evaporated, his body disappearing from between my thighs without moving an inch. I opened my eyes to find myself dressed, with the book that I was reading next to the bed. I bent to grab it convinced that it had been just another of my dreams, but the moment my hand reached the novel I also saw something very familiar. A small piece of black material that I had worn this morning as underwear lay there, ripped, next to the manuscript.

A feeling of anxiety took over me as I was finally putting two and two together. I figured some things out a while ago, but my rational side prevented me from acknowledging.

I can't believe that this is happening... That this is real!!! But most of all, I can't believe that this is happening to me.

A few moments later a set of footsteps brought me back to reality. This time they weren't heels, this time they were a man's steps. I could tell because the sound they made was much more dull than sharp.

They soon stopped somewhere in my direction. The squealed from the opening door made me remain still like a living stone statue.

The room darkened with his presence as every step he made towards me took me closer to my own downfall.

He was death and life merged together in a predator's body.

Strength and dominance oozed from his every pore. But it was something else too... Something more that made a cold chill flash through my body.

His beautiful absinthe green eyes captured the depths of time, making him irresistible, undeniable, but also *fatal.*

All of my instincts were telling me to leave as fast as I could, but there was something stronger that kept me frozen to the spot. An unspoken link from the dawn of time, brought me here, in this place, meant to fulfill my destiny.

He is the living dead that people whispered about while looking, with fear, out the window... *He is a vampire.*

Come!

He took a few steps towards me, assessing my every single feature while I stood there motionless under his control.

"You can breathe, Sarah!" he whispered so close to my neck that the sound of his voice vibrated in my ear. I then realized that even my breathing stopped in his presence.

I could finally see him up close, and the gallery light served him no justice. He was flawless. His strong jawline covered by a small stubble gave him a tidy unshaven look that only accentuated his masculinity. Every strand of his jet black hair was perfectly groomed. What am I talking about? *He is perfection!*

"I heard you calling me Sarah," he smirked while whispering once more, just inches from my mouth.

I could remember all too well the moment his name was evading my lips and my cheeks were turning red from that sweet recollection.

Who is this man? My body is slowly melting just from the sound of his voice. I fear what a single touch might do to me. Yes, I realize that there's something about Damien that links him to the man that I see every night. But knowing that this is reality, that I see him here before me with my very own eyes brings things to a whole different level.

I know he's a vampire and I'm not scared by that. Fascination is the only word to describe what I'm experiencing. I am nonetheless frightened by him as a man, by the control his presence can have over me, *subduing my heart and my body to his own will.*

He took a few steps, circling my body, analyzing me, just like I usually do with a new piece of art. Was I a new attraction for him? If so, please spare me the misery. Lay me down on the bed and attend my mortal needs.

"Why did you call for me?" he asked again touching the back of my neck with his lips. His whisper was so sensual that my skin formed goosebumps causing shivers to travel throughout my body.

My legs were failing me in his presence. My knees were turning into jelly while I could feel him so close to my skin.

"Mr. Arion," I managed to babble, incapable of forming a coherent sentence.

"Call me Damien as you did earlier. This is the name you will speak with desire from now on"- he murmured, returning in front of me.

This arrogant piece of... of... Shit, he was right. Desire is the only word to describe the feeling that emerges so strong just by looking his way. But for him just to blurt it out like that!!!

"*Come!*" he ordered and I obeyed, not subdued by some spell, but motivated purely by curiosity alone and let's be honest... fascination.

I followed him down the lobby that I had originally entered this room from, watching his whole body moving as he walked in front of me.

Broad shoulders and a muscular back were shifting under his black t-shirt. He didn't dress how I expected him to, elegant clothes like some lost prince. His casual look with a cotton t-shirt that allowed a few tattoos to peek from under the material and a ripped pair of jeans, made him even more attractive.

We finally reached the living room. He headed towards a leather couch that was situated close to the *mysterious* painting. Once there, he sat down, relaxed and waited for me to join him.

I reached his side and took a place on the sofa in front of him, waiting patiently for him to talk. I still wasn't convinced he was the same man that visited me every night, so I wasn't sure what to say.

"Would you like something to drink?" he asked, looking at me a little bit concerned because my face was probably changing colors.

"Water, please," I whispered since that was all I was capable of at that time.

"Water," he laughed standing up and heading towards a small house bar.

After a few moments of assessing some old bottles, he chose one and pored some red liquid in two crystal glasses.

Blood!!! If he thinks he's going to make me drink blood, he's crazy!!!

I almost jumped from my seat as he gently placed the glass in my hand, stroking my fingers as he closed them on the base of the glass.

"Drink, you'll feel much better," he ordered looking directly into my eyes.

I'm not drinking that! I said to myself as my hand was already pressing the glass on my lips.

No! No! No! I almost screamed as the blood was now flowing down my throat.

Funny...It tastes just like alcohol.

"Do you not like the wine I selected," he asked so casually that it almost drove me crazy.

*Wine...*relax Sarah, it's just wine.

"For someone who is looking to convince me of something you're very quiet," he took a sip from his glass, laying back on the couch.

I had even forgotten what I was here for! I had been so caught up with uncovering Damien's secrets that I lost track of my initial plan... And he had definitely noticed that.

"I'm sorry, I came here this morning fully prepared, but I think my fatigue has really got to me. However, this won't be a problem." I confidently looked directly in his eyes, trying to regain some part of myself back. "I and the gallery that I represent would be very interested in working with you. Whether this collaboration would be to simply provide you with new pieces of art, or help you dispose of some of your old ones, we would be more than happy to spare you the time spent on achieving that"- the words of a professional.

He looked at me like he didn't believe a word I said, smiled and took another sip from his glass.

"Miss Audrey is here to see you!"- the woman that let me in earlier came straight up to Damien and spoke loudly, just like she was letting me know that I'm just a name on tonight's guest list.

He first looked at me, sensing my discomfort as I always had difficulty in hiding my emotions. I don't know yet why, but this was affecting me in just the same way as the heels I had heard early in the lobby.

"Send her away," he ordered, returning the glass to his lips and emptying it.

"Margaret, prepare dinner for two then leave," he spoke as the woman was heading towards the entrance door.

"Of course Sir," she replied politely, with a completely different tone than the one that she used when speaking with me.

"Excuse me for a second," he threw me a faded smile, got up and left the room.

I nodded. Honestly, I didn't mind, even though the lack of his presence was leaving me somewhat empty, but, his simple posture is so imposing that it gives me difficulties in acting normally.

I finished my drink. I still can't believe that I thought it was blood. My imagination must be running wild again, but one thing I knew for sure: *he is a vampire*!

I started thinking about the number of women that visit him every night. A hollow sensation formed in my stomach. I was having very mixed feelings. I felt both disgusted but in a strange way jealous as well. Was I jealous that I wasn't one of them or that they're touching something that belongs to me? I wasn't sure, such funny thoughts!

He belonging to me.

Where is Lala to wake me up to reality when I need her to?

I got up, and an old Chinese vase drew my attention. This must be the artifact Karla was talking about, but who keeps a 10 million vase in their apartment?

I carefully went over to look at it. I wouldn't dream of touching it. I can only imagine the anxiety his housekeeper feels while dusting it. It was beautiful. You could actually feel the passing of time just looking at it. Even though it was a simple white vase with blue painting, it was so special.

"Beautiful, isn't it?" Damien spoke as he returned to the room.

"I'm assuming you aren't interested in selling it," I chuckled.

"I have difficulty parting with things I like," he answered seductively while heading towards the table to take my empty glass.

"It didn't seem so earlier. You didn't even give a second thought on sending your visitor away." **Stupid Sarah, just stupid, why did you say something like that???**

He didn't answer and went to the bar and silently refilled our glasses as my stupid words echoed in my mind.

After he finished, he slowly approached me and placed the refreshed glass in my hand, but this time keeping his hand over mine whilst pulling me closer to him.

"If I didn't know better, I'd say you were jealous," his words recoiled off the skin of my neck, imprinting themselves on my brain.

"And who said I liked my visitor," he continued, soothing a little of my concerns.

I couldn't face him, so I looked away, only to see the *other him.*

My eyes lingered on his painting, admiring again it's perfection.

"You like that?" he asked, standing behind me so I could have a clearer view.

"I don't usually keep portraits, but this one was a present. A friend gave it to me," he grazed his lips on my neck while speaking.

"A 300-year-old friend." Yes, it's a fact! My stupid mouth just can't keep itself shut.

He turned me around and placed both hands on my shoulders, caught my eyes with his own and spoke:-

"Yes, Sarah! A 300-year-old friend!"

Hunter

He was admitting it?!?!? I said to myself as soon as he answered.

Was I scared that he found out about my suspicions? A little. I was much more interested to find out other things about him. I didn't want to seem too intrusive but there was a certain question that needed elucidation.

"What are you?" I asked, unable to control my curiosity.

"Don't ask questions you already know the answer to" he growled, letting one of his fangs show slightly, then quickly returned to the couch.

Should I run? Head through the door, go straight home, maybe move to another city? That's certainly what any normal person would do. But not me. My destiny was pulling me towards him with every word he spoke and my fascination for him was sewing an *unseen thread.*

With small steps, I headed towards the sofa and took my former spot, right in front of him.

"Why are you here, Sarah?" he asked, a little irritated this time.

"To get you to work with our gallery. The truth is that my job is depending on this, so I can't leave here with NO for an answer"- I was determined to get that deal tonight.

"Am I getting the same advantages Augusto did?" he doubtfully asked. *Was that....**jealousy**?*

"I'm not sure what you're implying, but I assure you that no job is important enough so that I could sell my body." I muttered as I stood up, offended by his remark.

In just one second he was next to me. "I didn't mean to offend you. I was just curious about what this implied." His finger ran up my arm the same way Augusto had a few days ago. The only difference was that this time I didn't try to pull away.

I was smart enough to figure out he wasn't hitting on me. This was a test to see how my body responded next to his in comparison to the way it had rejected the Italian businessman. *This was jealousy!*

"Since I'm not selling, what can you offer me to purchase?" he asked, but not in an offending manner to my surprise.

"I have more than enough paintings. I'm much more interested in art objects these days, 17th-century max. What came after that you could hardly worth calling art." At least we both agree on something.

"I'm sure that we have several objects that you may find interesting." I stated proudly. In my mind I was already browsing through the list of artifacts I could present him from our inventory.

"What I usually want you can't get from the art dealers market. I'm more of a lost treasure hunter," he smiled, tracing the back of his index finger from my cheekbone to my lips.

He was definitely a **hunter**, I noticed that with his every single gesture but I've decided to show him that I'm not the 'lost deer' he's looking for.

"I'm more than determined to find these special art pieces for you. We do have a serious list of clients that sell their collections only through private auctions. I'm sure that we can find something to satisfy your cravings." I took a few steps back placing a small distance between us. I usually don't play games with clients, but apparently, Damien needs that 'special treatment'.

"I'm referring to your art cravings, Mr. Arion. Business only!" I crossed my arms and put my full professional mask on.

"I intend to dedicate all my working time to this contract, if you would agree to it of course."

"Aren't you afraid of me, Sarah?" he asked, closing the distance between us once again, defying my professional attitude.

"Should I be, Mr. Arion?" I inquired without flinching.

"I told you to call me Damien, and yes, you should! It's in my nature to hurt people, even though those aren't always my intentions." He spoke with a hint of sadness in his voice that resonated right through my soul.

Was it regret or worry? But what could a man like him be worried about?

"Have dinner with me!" he ordered walking towards the bar and refilled his glass.

He suddenly became pale, placing a hand on the counter to support his weight. His arm was slowly shaking as he put the glass to his lips and emptied it within a single sip. He then looked at me, and I could notice a shade of red covering the absinthe in his eyes. His chest was rising with increasing speed, his breathing intensified and his beautiful face was shifting as if in pain.

"Sarah" he whispered with the voice I longed to hear, shattering all illusions that I could leave this house without being hopelessly in love with him.

His nails gouged the counter, leaving deep marks in their path while his fangs were emerging and retreating as if he was trying to fight it.

I was no longer important. I was scared for whatever was happening to him and only felt able to start breathing again after his skin color began to return to normal.

He poured another glass, took a sip and walked past me as he left through a large black wooden door.

"Come"- he barked and I followed blindly, led by his words.

A massive wooden 16th-century dinner table stood in the middle of the room. The walls were decorated with a Victorian black wallpaper, very similar to the one in the living room.

If I could count properly, I think it was a 16-setting table, carefully arranged with fine flatware and crystal glasses, as if at any moment the room could be filled with people who will be served dinner.

Everything was perfectly laid out, just like a movie set. Not even a napkin was out of place.

"Please, take a seat," he gently ushered me, pulling a seat from the end of the table.

I slowly walked towards him with small steps, trying to find an algorithm before I reached his side, to restrict my ardor for his touch.

In slow-motion, I positioned myself at the table while he adjusted my chair, not without brushing his lips on my shoulder before he walked to the head of the table to take his seat.

I wasn't sure what to say. The atmosphere was thick with the unspoken attraction between us. It was making it difficult for me to sit still in my place since the turmoil between my thighs was beginning to visibly bother me.

He didn't speak a word, but I could feel his eyes scanning my body from across the room. The only thing that I was concerned about was, is this just pure curiosity for him or something more?

This is most probably only in my imagination, but still... Is there the slightest chance that his eyes are betraying him the same way my body does?

Margaret stepped into the room bringing us dinner. "Balsamic glazed roast beef with vegetables," the woman proudly announced as if she was presenting her finest creation. Then she looked at us until Damien nodded his approval and a smile appeared on her face.

She made her way to a cabinet and poured us two glasses of red wine. My eyes were captured by Damien's aura that seemed to be carefully weaving a net of desire around me.

"You can go home!", he calmly ordered. The woman bowed her head and left through the door, immediately after placing the wine glasses in front of us.

Damien searched his pockets for the phone, then after tapping the screen a few times, turned on some music. No Adams Family pipe organ, I guess.

We served dinner in a very elegant manner as if we were both at a luxury restaurant, carefully arranging every piece on our plates.

After a few bites, my mind was gradually drifting not only to the moments spent in the guest room but also to all of Damien's gestures... the way he had held my hand, the way he whispered in my ear and brushed his lips against my skin.

I could actually feel how my breasts started to ache for his touch, swelling underneath my dress, while I was stirring in my seat, trying to clasp my legs as hard as I could to withstand the storm that was forming below my waist. What is he doing to me? I have never been this aroused without being touched in my whole life!

"Fuck, Sarah!" he growled hard, making the walls vibrate with his words.

In a sip he emptied the glass, put his plates aside and cleared the counter in front of him.

"Come, please!" he looked directly in my eyes then at the table, while pushing himself and his chair almost a meter back.

Call it madness, but I got up and headed towards his end of the table with few hopes of be stilling my heart. This wasn't a spell it was my very own will.

I leaned on the counter, facing Damien who's look was now fixated below my waist.

With one move, he reached and pulled the massive wooden table until I was forced to get on the table cloth.

His breathing was heavy, resting his hands on my knees, leaving me to swallow the lump in my throat.

His palms started traveling up my thighs, underneath my dress while his eyes were feeding on my reactions.

My lips were trembling, and entwining my tongue around his was the first thing that came to my mind. He smirked like he knew what I was thinking, then lifted my dress just a little.

With one swift move, he yanked me over from the table, making me land on his crotch where my core collided with his hardness.

"Fuck!" he cursed again, pulling my head to his shoulder and burying his face in my hair, right above my collarbone.

He didn't move for a few minutes like he was trying to collect himself, but I could feel him twitching beneath me and that only heightened my eagerness further.

"Wear panties next time, I can hardly contain myself," he muttered spending a few more moments next to my neck.

I gasped, angry that he would talk to me that way, but I was also lost in the eroticism of the moment.

"Sarah" he whispered our lips barely touching, placing his forehead on mine and coping my face with his hands. "What are you doing here?"

"I... I came for the contract."

"I must warn you that I don't appreciate being lied to. **The truth, Sarah!** Why are you here?" his tone was much more menacing than before, even frightening I must admit.

I was not only surprised at what was happening between us but how fast things were evolving- "For the gallery... The contract!" I blabbered, also realizing that it's a mistake.

"Very well!" he calmly spoke, lifting me up on my feet and rearranging my skirt.

"The contract!" He said rising from the chair and taking a few steps in the opposite direction.

"You can inform your boss that you've got yourself a new client.

After all, I can't deny you of anything you want." He talked with a bitter sadness in his voice.

"All transactions will be done by email so that we don't have to physically meet"- words that cut deep into my soul, but this is what I wanted from my visit here... *Right*?

"Let me walk you to the door. I just remembered that I have a business meeting that I can't revoke."

We stepped towards the door while I thought a million times of giving him a different answer, but I couldn't. With a faded smile he whispered while closing the door behind me:

"It was the right choice, Sarah!"

Regrets

After the Gala

Damien

I drove off in a hurry, trying to put a distance between the monster inside and the first woman ever to leave me powerless.

My body was almost boiling. Even though the blood I've consumed tonight would normally last me a few days, I was still devoured by hunger... *I was hungry for her!*

I came back to my apartment and sank into the silence of my room. It was so quiet that I could hear my inner self scream for her presence.

My eyes closed and my thoughts immediately raced towards her, as my soul found Sarah once again in the darkness of her room. Contrary to what other people believe vampires do sleep, at least in a trance like state that allows our bodies to rest while our senses are still alert. Just like a self-defense mechanism.

My desires, my lusts, my hopes all merged together and took the path that leads me to Sarah. My soul visits her every night. Even though I'm not fully in control, I experience every single sensation, every breath, every touch.

I started dreaming about Sarah almost two years ago. I knew even then that the possibility of her being the one I was searching for really existed. I tried denying it at first. Drowning myself in the blood of countless women, thinking that this is another figment of my fantasy, some hidden desire that had been accumulating with the passing of centuries. But she is for real and my soul couldn't stay away from her own.

Even though I could never see her face in my dreams before, I know it's her. The softness of her skin is impregnated in my mind like a pattern that's been there all along. Such a strong attraction that my lips can't resist devouring Sarah's body the second my soul reaches the chamber she's in.

This night is different from all the others. Her calling sounds louder than before and our destinies can no longer be kept for intertwining.

I'm eager to experience each touch as my body closes in on hers and my lips consume the side of her neck.

I'm burning and there's nothing to stop me now! My soul can no longer be contained, it will not be able to find peace until it owns *hers*.

I slowly lift Sarah's shirt, making her groan in anticipation, as she pushed herself back a little, closing the distance between us. My kisses lead me to her earlobe as her breath becomes heavy and her body surrenders itself to me. My tongue pushed her lips to part, claiming her sweet mouth as mine.

This was something different than I had never experienced before. Every centimeter of my body was screaming for Sarah and the desire for us to become as one surpassed every other though.

Small moans were echoing from her mouth as I removed her shirt, leaving me the site of her perfect naked body.

I know that there's something special about Sarah, not only is she my destiny, but there's something more. She's not a normal human being and that makes things a thousand times more dangerous. But, still, I can't help myself and I whisper my deepest secret. "Te astept de asa mult timp" (*I've been waiting for so long*).

My lips crashed on her silken breasts. My mouth has waited many centuries to taste her soft skin, but it was all worth it.

The way her body twitched with each swirl of my tongue over her throbbing tips was driving me insane. Even though I tried to prolong these moments as much as I could, her sweet moans and the movement of her body made it impossible for me to wait any longer.

I placed myself between her thighs and returned to that sweet mouth, pushing her lips to part. This time she took me by surprise and anxiously responded to my kiss, twisting her tongue against my own while her hips moved around my waist, forcing me to lose all strength.

My mouth traveled, eagerly consuming her breasts, lustful and ravaged by hunger. The room in my pants became too small and I needed to escape from this clothing prison.

Once freed, I placed myself next to her core, listening to her shallow breathing. I could tell she was nervous but also impatient at the same time for us to be united.

Only seconds kept us from experiencing the extreme pleasures we sought after but I felt something burning on my skin. I shifted my gaze for a second to see a ray of light grazing my arm. My soul immediately reacted, shattering my trance and bringing me back to my room that was now so empty without her.

My stomach was actually hurting from a hunger never suffered before, making my hands begin to shake. I found myself in desperate need to reach out for a supply of blood.

I hate drinking blood if it is not directly from a human, but right now there was no time. The beast inside was fighting to be released, and who knows what uncountable damage it could have done. I felt like I just found water after traveling weeks in the desert. But what bothered me the most was that I felt weak and that's *the last thing that defines me.*

She stirs a fire so deep inside that all my other emotions fuse into a feeling that starts to dominate my very being. I wanted her close, but I also wanted her as far away as possible. I know what my life has to offer and I would ***never*** want that for her.

In the first centuries after I was transformed, I thought the world was mine to conquer. The thirst for blood made me feared amongst humans and my ambitions brought me respect from the other ones of my kind.

There was always a battle for supremacy on this world, and my stubbornness almost led me to erase all of mankind... if *someone* hadn't stopped me.

We are not so different from humans. We all crave money, power, respect, but our ambitions are greater. *My ambitions were greater!* Driven by a need to be on top of it all, I managed to create my own army. In just a few years vampire numbers had almost equaled the humans.

I made a mistake! Blinded by power, I almost killed the world I was born into until a pure soul showed me the way. But that was a long time ago and my memories conjoin with the passing of time to the point where I can't even remember her face.

Did I love her? I don't know. Maybe I was too young, maybe the games of power were too big back then, but one thing I do know, she saved me! She saved me so that I could destroy her!

I represent death in its purest form. Everything I am, from the way I move my lips as I talk to the sound my footsteps make while approaching my unsuspecting victim. Every little detail is made to draw them in, subdue their minds to the spell of my presence.

I can't deny that this existence brought me great perks. The sick feeling that you can control someone's whole life just by speaking a few words still feeds my inner monster, not the vampire, *the real me.*

The fortune I raised, the knowledge I collected over time, they all had a cost. The price of all the sunshine's spent behind closed doors, all the people buried along the way. A solitude that isn't wanted, but must be imposed is the only life I know now.

I live in my own silence, undisturbed by the world outside. Sure, I have different women that accompany me through the nights. Time must be consumed some way, why wouldn't it be a pleasant one? I do like to play with my food, just like a cat plays with a mouse, the only difference between us is that my prey always returns begging for more.

I can still feel the thirst for absolute power, to rule them all again, because this time I would know exactly what to do. But I smother it every time, by remembering the capacity of my destruction.

My hunger had calmed a little and even though I know that another encounter with her would bring me once again to my limit, I secretly yearn for it. Maybe I should try to practice more will power, but until a few hours ago it didn't betray me.

More than a couple of centuries passed since my fangs controlled my being. I'm stronger than that, and I will take all precautions to ensure that this never happens again.

A knock on the door takes me away from my thoughts- "Enter!"

The woman that had served me for more than a decade makes her way into my room.

I met Margaret when I first came to New York. During the first years she earned my trust. She isn't the only human that shares my secret, but she's the only one I don't have to control to keep quiet.

"Sir, you have a visitor."

The Count

Agnes stepped into the room, filling the air around her with a sweet, but overwhelming perfume. I really despise women that in their attempt to be perfect, cross over the limit and stroll into a ridiculous level... A little too much makeup, a little too much perfume, and a little too few clothes. She was definitely one of those. Probably spending two hours in front of a mirror before leaving her apartment in her failed attempt to make me choose her.

I would lie if I said that she wasn't an attractive woman. Her perky breasts hiding beneath her dress and a pair of toned long legs allowed her to spend a few nights in my room, but I have a feeling that she and all other entertainers will soon belong to a forgotten past.

"Damien" she whispered taking a seat on my bed and taking her jacket off.

"We're going out!" I muttered, heading towards the door. I have no intention to end the night how she was imagining. I could hear her steps behind me as she tried to catch up, but I was at the parking lot before she managed to reach me.

I drove off without saying a word the whole way, trying to recollect my thoughts. There was something that was worrying me. A certain disgust at the thought of touching another woman besides Sarah was slowly taking control and the ladies that usually helped me occupy my time were no longer a *viable* solution.

I stopped the car in from of my favorite club. Discretion is the word that rules this place and it's probably the only zone around here in which vampires can find willing people to serve them as dinner.

My friend Adam owns this location, and since he has a weird sense of humor, he named it "The Count." Hiding in plain sight apparently is the best strategy in his opinion. I can't help but be amused by the absurdity of the situation.

He found a way to intermediate the relationships between humans and vampires, making them donate their blood for different rewards. Most of them want money, but there are some who do it for the thrill. The endorphins released while feeding give a certain addiction and there are a few regulars hooked on that. Usually, my meals want a little pleasure on the side. I can't complain, but I always end up being forced to end the relationship using my power of conviction. Every single woman that went through my bed lived with the hope that she would be the last.

" Damien, my old, old friend" - Adam's voice came from behind me in his attempt to annoy me.

"I think you're much older than me. For all I know, you could be Eve's Adam." I muttered taking a whiskey bottle from the bar behind him and filling myself a glass.

"The mortals drink, there's definitely something wrong! Miss, can I lead you to a table, I need to catch up with my friend for a while. I promise you'll have him back in a moment." Adam politely asked Agnes to leave, noticing that my current state of mind was also pushing me to send her away.

I found her, I whispered the second he was back, making him stop in front of a chair and start laughing.

"Who Damien? *Your half*?! I think you already drank too much."

"Fuck Adam, I'm not in the mood for your sarcasm. The dreams were true!"

"Ok. First of all, I've been around this place since *forever* and I didn't manage to find a *half*". I'm not even sure such a thing exists except in books and TV shows. Secondly, you lived for almost a thousand years, maybe you're lonely and see one of your dinners as the missing piece of your life." Adam started laughing making me unable to control my anger. My hand reached his throat and threw him on the wall next to the bar, making the bricks that decorated it shatter.

Another vampire tried to stop me, but I was in killing mode. The second I felt his hand on my arm trying to keep me in my place, I turned and sunk my fangs into his neck.

"Stop!" Adam screamed, pulling me away before I could rip his jugular.

"Damien, look at me!"- he commanded grabbing a glass of blood from the bar's countertop and placing it in my hands.

He waited for me to finish consuming it, managing this way to still my inner beast for a while.

"I guess you weren't kidding!" he muttered while signaling the staff to clean the place up and return to normal.

"I have trouble with self-control", I admitted to him. The chances were that he already noticed that while colliding with the brick wall.

Adam looked at me for a few seconds "I don't understand. You're the most composed person I ever met. You could be a Buddhist for all I know."

"She's not just my half, she wakes my inner beast. Her blood is all I can think about".

" So, turn her and live happily ever after. Or are you afraid of spending an eternity with the same person? I know I would be." Adam started laughing again, but my next words made his face change color "Adam, she's an *Amplifier*!"

"Now I know you had something to drink before you got here!"

I didn't have the time or the temper for his nonsense, so I took my glass and headed towards my table.

"Wait!" he ran after me. "You weren't kidding. Did she choose sides yet?"

"I don't think so, but I can't know for sure. I only saw her for a minute".

"You're in deep shit, my friend. Let's go into my office for a while."

I followed Adam to the dungeon he called his office. I guess old habits die hard.

"You could have renovated this place in the last two or three centuries." I muttered, a little uncomfortable, remembering the times that we actually kept human prisoners in very similar places to this one in order to feed my armies.

"This is renovated! The club's built in the '50s, but I missed the old days, so I made it look like home. Plus, I have some volunteers in here from time to time."

I interrupted Adam, thinking more about what I had on my mind "I think I need to leave town, go to Italy or France for a while, at least until things cool down."

"The mighty Damien is running. I never thought that I would live to see the day, neither did I want to. I actually think that you should learn how to control it, and I have an idea just how to start."

"You do?!" I asked, surprised because I didn't come here searching for answers, just searching for an old friend.

"Do you ever feel more satisfied or fuller after feeding on a certain person?" he asked, trying to get to a certain point.

"Yes, I think we all do. I'm guessing it has something to do with the blood type."

"Precisely! And since I plan to open a luxury blood store, I have the perfect solution for you. AB4!"

"That's pretty rare."

"Yes, only 0.6 percent of human population shares it. The funny fact is that it's very common amongst serial killers and psychopaths. I recently discovered that this precise blood group acts as a very powerful nutrient for us. Drinking it as a regular meal would leave you satisfied for up to 10 times longer than normal blood."

"So, I could control my urges much more efficiently."

"Exactly. I do suggest some training before you encounter the girl from your dreams or *of your dreams*" he smirked, annoying the hell out of me.

"I'm not going to see her!"

"Damien, you should have learned by now: *fate doesn't take our plans into consideration*."

"Just give me the fucking bottles to try and I will see if it works." I muttered, already frustrated by his sense of humor. I'm usually not like this when it comes to Adam, but I really need to convince myself if this works or not.

"How many cradles should I load in your car?"

"All that you have!" I answered, already thinking of a plan on how to push the limits.

"You owe me a small fortune. Business before friendship," he reminded me, and I know he wasn't kidding.

"I'll write you a check. Tell them to load them now!" I walked through the office door directly to the club determined to find Agnes.

"Oh... Leaving already." Adam's joyful laughter echoed from behind me. Money was his favorite thing in the world. I think he would even sell his immortality for the right price.

"We're leaving!" I command the moment I reached her table, then turned away and walked to the car.

"Where are we going? Did something happen?" she asked running after me.

"Let's just say that I have *different plans* for tonight!"

Blood

As I drove towards my place Agnese's hand suddenly rested on my thigh, then slid slowly between my legs "Pull over" she whispered, licking her lips and leaning in for a kiss. I wasn't in the mood for her games "Stay in your place!" I growled, smothering the small drop of personality she might have had.

I continued driving, unimpressed by her pouting. She wasn't some girlfriend that I had to comfort, she was just a way to a means for me. And right now, that means is self-control.

We reached my apartment and I decided to put my new plan to use, even though my company for the night didn't seem to get the message. As I was opening a bottle of the newly discovered treasure, her hands started finding their way underneath my shirt from back to front, examining my every muscle.

"Enough!" I screamed swinging my arm and accidentally throwing her on the couch.

"Go to my room! Now!" This girl wasn't testing my self-control for drinking her blood, she was testing my patience!

Fortunately for her, she, complied in just a second and my urge to end her was pacified.

I poured myself a glass of the blood and tasted its flavor. I had this type of blood before but never noticed that it had properties other than a sweet taste. Come to think about it, I was never before in this situation, almost blinded by a person's simple presence.

Convinced that it's time, I headed towards my bedroom, ready to feed on Agnese's blood.

She was waiting for me on the bed and her dress seemed to have evaporated since some red lace lingerie was the only thing that was covering her body. I could see the excitement in her eyes as I approached her. *If she would only know my real plans.*

My fangs went straight to her neck, ripping her skin to only take a few sips and to make sure I gave her some of my endorphins so she can resist what's to come.

I retreated, leaving her confused about what was happening.

"Just wait!" I commanded before she could drive me crazy with another question and make me end this sooner than planned.

Her eyes were now giving me a seductive plead as the endorphins were taking control, making her hips grind on the silk sheet. However, none of this impressed me. I was far too busy looking straight at the wound I had just made and at how drops of blood were rolling from her skin down on the bed.

Useless! I still had full control. I need to push further, so I approach her again, biting the upper part of her breast and making another incision.

Still not enough! I had to continue, leaving marks all over her body, and then waited for my inner monster to have a reaction.

I was now looking at more than a dozen open wounds and the blood that was shooting out of them didn't impress me at all. In normal circumstances, this would have an effect on me. I would still be able to control myself, but I would have to fight the desire of drinking more.

This could only mean one thing. Adam must have been right. This type of blood is more consistent and could help me remain in control in case of an unplanned encounter.

I stood there next to the bed, looking at Agnese's body for a few hours. She was too busy drifting away from the endorphins. I was so convinced that this could work when an unstoppable hunger came over me.

I could barely leave the bedside to reach the blood bottle and take a few sips.

I needed a few minutes to regain my strengths. Even though the new blood seemed to have the effect of calming me down, something was off. I wasn't hungry for Agnese's blood. A much sweeter scent invaded my senses and the familiarity of it almost left me breathless.

It was Sarah's! But how could that be possible? Maybe it's from this restraint I'm trying, I must have pushed myself a little too hard.

"Mr. Arion," Margaret's voice echoed from the lobby. "You have a visitor," she continued her sentence confirming my suspicions. But how could that be possible?

My judgment was still a little clouded, and even though Margaret has seen this sort of thing while working for me, I wasn't going to let her witness Agnes covered in her own blood.

"What is she doing here?" I asked, leaving the room and closing the door behind me.

"She didn't tell me, but how do you know who your visitor is?" she was surprised since I can't feel people from such a great distance, but, with Sarah, it's all different.

"I just know!" I growled, unwilling to give Margaret any explanations regarding my senses.

"I'm sorry I pried, should I send her away?" she stuttered, knowing that it was not the moment to get on my bad side.

"No, ask her to wait in one of the guest's rooms. I can't see her right now."

She nodded, returning to the living room to follow my instructions.

I knew this was a bad decision, but it was the only one my heart allowed me to make. Somehow my lust managed to convince my brain that this could be a test of endurance and since nothing can stand in my way, I was determined not to let this opportunity pass it.

I could feel her walking towards her chamber and with each step that touched the marble floor, the knot in my stomach grew larger. I could hardly persuade myself not to break the walls apart to be reunited with her. I was by now in both physical and also spiritual pain.

I pulled out a chair and sat on it, waiting for the storm inside of me to calm. I needed to force myself to accommodate her presence, so I started with short breaths, filling my lungs with her scent.

My eyes were fixated on the bed where Agnes lay, still in her own paradise. The blood that was covering her presented absolutely no attraction to me, come to think about it, *I could bathe in rivers of blood and I would still crave hers.*

I poured myself another glass, then after drinking it, took a towel from the bathroom and cleaned Agnes. Her presence was now useless, just torture reminding me that I could have any woman besides the one I truly desire.

"Wake up!" I muttered the second I was done, and she did exactly that.

"Leave!" I barked, annoyed by her somehow seductive gaze. She didn't even flinch but, put her clothes on and left through the door.

Finally, alone, I lay on the bed already thinking about solutions that could make me be close to her, and not ones to push her away.

I was surprised at how quickly she managed to change my heart without even seeing her. I am undoubtedly a strong man, but I just found my biggest weakness.

I wasn't planning on drifting off, but my restless soul couldn't control itself. The second my eyes closed I left to go to her room.

Even if I wasn't fully in control, it did express my every single desire and I could experience each touch. The moment it reached the chamber, I saw her perfect body lying on the bed as her closeness in real-life drove my soul to its very limits.

I could feel my hands tangling her hair with a pure hunger of possessing every piece of her body.

With one move I was between Sarah's hips, lifting her dress up so that I could feel her core pressing directly on me. I kissed her with a devastating urge. *So animalistic, so pure, so complete!*

My hands traveled towards her breasts, but the dress was an unwanted obstacle in my search to explore the satin skin in front of me. The moment that it was gone, I pinned her hands on the pillows above her head, ordering them to stay still, strapping them with invisible bonds.

I moved to Sarah's breasts, removing her bra and kissed and lightly bit her quivering tips that were almost calling out for my lips to taste them.

I could feel her breaths became shorter waiting eagerly for my next move, while her hips fastened against my waist.

I now controlled Sarah's senses and her body. The idea that I could dominate every second of her life through all eternity aroused me more than any other human attraction ever could. Soon, my fangs emerged. But I was able to distract myself, ripping the small piece of material that was covering her soft skin.

My fingers started grinding between her folds. Her excitement built and was hard to contain, at least for my sensitive senses. I quickly picked up the increasing pounding of her heart and the faded scent of her arousal. I wanted to bring things to a new level.

My kisses descended on her body, from her chest to her abdomen, then right between the thighs, claiming her nub.

My hand was still there, attending to her desires, but I think, it was not enough anymore. I slide one of my fingers inside her, provoking her hips to press firmly into the mattress.

My hand matched the pace of my tongue, taking her close to the edge with just a few movements.

I slipped another finger into her and slowly swirled them, making sure I reached that special spot that'll make her toes curl.

Her pleasure was now my own and I was eager to see her in ecstasy.

She didn't fail me, and a few minutes after her body spasmed under my touch, making my name leave her lips.

"Damien," her shallow breath managed to carry my name from her lips, carving this moment into the history of my life, like one I desired to repeat each day.

My eyes opened and I was again in my bed, intoxicated by the taste of her.

Her calling my name must have snapped me away from my dream, bringing me back to the real world. I was a little frustrated because I didn't have more fantasy time with Sarah, but also eager to leave this room and reach her.

Now, after knowing her sweetness, I was more than determined to turn this dream into a *reality*

Sneak into my soul

I drank a few glasses from the newly purchased bottle. Then, after calming down a little, I decided to finally see her.

I'm not sure why she came, or what excuse brought her to my doorstep, but one thing is clear, destiny is setting the cards and only we could choose how to play them.

I opened her chamber door with a certain fear that I won't be able to control myself, but my senses were now a little calmer than before.

She was standing next to the bed, still a little flustered from our recent dream she just shared. Her big eyes looking straight at the door.

Her lower lip was trembling more and more with each step I took. I'm not sure if it was fear or excitement, but it certainly had an effect on me. Seeing her reaction to my approach fueled my ego. The power I had over her brought me both great satisfaction and excitement. The urge to see her every response under my touch was so agonizingly high in my thoughts that I was in serious danger of letting the monster free.

"You can breathe," I whispered, knowing that I'll only intensify her restlessness.

"I heard you calling me Sarah," I continue, letting her know that her little secret is out.

I took a few steps, circling around her, without stopping my curiosity from studying her beautiful features up close.

"Why did you call for me?" I asked again, not being able to keep myself from resting my lips on the back of her neck.

"Mr. Arion," her voice was trembling, betraying her weaknesses.

"Call me Damien, as you did earlier. This is the name you will speak with desire from now on," I demanded, stepping in front of her so that I can look directly into her eyes.

She needs to know who's in control, to whom she truly belongs to.

"*Come!*" I asked her to follow me to the living room. We had to leave that room as I was finding it impossible to contain myself from getting dangerously close to her.

Once there, I offered her a drink, making sure that I get the chance to pour myself a glass of the new blood while she wasn't looking.

I'm so certain that she suspects something's wrong but I'm not aware how much she knows. Seeing me drink blood, even from a glass, wasn't on today's goals list.

"For someone who wants to convince me of something, you're very quiet," I spoke to her as I lay on the couch enjoying my liquor and trying to calm down.

She answered me, but I'm not sure exactly what she said because I was too busy keeping my fangs out of sight. All I remember is that she mumbled something about her work, but I knew her true reasons for coming here are much more related to her heart than to her job.

"Miss Audrey is here to see you!" Margaret announced. She is one of my regular blood suppliers, but the involuntary look of sadness that spread on Sarah's face made me gasp.

"Send her away," I ordered, finishing the last of my drink. The thought of Audrey's blood had lost its appeal, but the thought of drinking directly from a vein had not. My eyes were fixated on Sarah while my mind became a little clouded.

"Margaret, prepare dinner for two, then leave." I turned my attention to the other part of the living room, hoping I could get past these moments.

"Excuse me for a second." I got up with my last strength and moved towards my room. The second I unlocked the door I opened another bottle of blood. I started drinking straight from it until my breathing had finally returned to normal and my senses calmed down.

It's funny how I feel like I'm always standing on an edge when around her. With each passing moment the adrenaline of being there becomes one of my guilty pleasures.

I returned to the living room with increased confidence, to find her studying one of my favorite artifacts. "Beautiful, isn't it?".

"I'm assuming you aren't interested in selling it" she left out a soft chuckle.

"I have great difficulties parting with things I like," and I meant it. Since she's definitely of my liking. I wouldn't mind having her locked up in my room for a century or two. These thoughts made me refill my glass sooner than I planned, but not before making sure that her glass is filled too with wine, not blood.

"It didn't seem so earlier when you didn't even give a second thought about sending your visitor away." There was a certain annoyance in her tone.

"If I didn't know better, I'd say you were jealous." I whispered while placing the wine glass in her hand and pulling her small body closer to mine.

"And who said I liked my visitor?" the truth was I couldn't even look at someone else while she was in the same room.

Her eyes were trying to avoid mine. She focused her attention towards a portrait of me carried out by a very old friend of mine "You like that?".

"I don't usually keep portraits, but this one was a present. A good friend gave it to me." I continued while brushing my lips on the skin of her neck. I love the way this forms goosebumps letting me know that she also wants me, even if I am playing Russian roulette with myself.

"A 300-year-old friend," she surprised me with her boldness, making me aware of her suspicions.

The devil inside needed to see her face as I confessed. I got in front of her and slowly grabbed her shoulders. Making sure that she was looking directly at me, "Yes, Sarah! A 300-year-old friend!"

"What are you?" a whisper of her voice reached my ears.

"Don't ask questions you already know the answer to." I muttered letting one of my fangs be seen, a little annoyed that now the element of surprise is gone.

I then headed towards the couch. To my surprise she followed me, taking a seat on the sofa in front of me.

"Why are you here, Sarah?" I asked, still irritated by the fact that she must see me as a monster now.

"To get you to work with our gallery. The truth is that my job is depending on this, so I can't leave here with NO for an answer," this little fox thinks that she can ever convince me to do something that I don't want to. I'll let her play her cards while I play mine and try to get the real answer out of her before the night ends.

"Am I getting the same advantages Augusto did?" I doubtfully asked, remembering the way he was touching her. The plain memory of that scum was making my blood boil.

"I'm not sure what you're implying, but I assure you that no job is important enough so that I could sell my body," she retaliated. I was thinking more about a mutual exchange amongst other things. I do admit that my desires are deeper than normal people's.

In one second, I was next to her, brushing my index on her arm the same way Augusto did. I was testing her every reaction "I didn't want to offend you I was just curious about what this implied."

I needed proof that my touch can't be compared with any other man's, and she didn't fail to confirm. Her body didn't even move, embracing my gesture like she had waited her whole life just to feel me.

Useless words were passed between us while my finger traveled from her cheek to her rose lips. My only wish was that *my* lips replaced it.

Even now she tried to maintain a professional attitude. Still hoping to convince me to work with her.

"Aren't you afraid of me Sarah?" I asked, closing the distance between us in my desire to feel her as close as I could.

"Should I be, Mr. Arion?" she asked doubtfully, crossing her arms.

"I told you to call me Damien, and yes, you should be! It's in my nature to hurt people, even though those aren't always my intentions." The mistakes of my past were still haunting me. I would give the last drop of life left in me so that I would never repeat them again.

"Have dinner with me!" I commanded heading towards the bar to have another glass of blood. Even though I tried to stop myself, my thoughts carried me to a dark place. Sometimes *my past comes back to haunt me* in the worst possible moments.

My fangs weren't listening to me anymore as an internal fight with myself began. My nails scratched the counter as the pain of controlling my monster was almost unbearable.

The blood soon had its effect on me as my human side finally began winning.

 I poured myself another glass just to make sure that the scene from earlier doesn't repeat itself.

"Come," growled, heading towards the dining room.

"Please, take a seat." I showed her to her place and pulled out a chair so that she can make herself comfortable. I may be a killer, but I still have manners. I came from the days where people still had respect for one another, even if I'm always the one respected. I know how to treat a woman when needed.

I took my seat at the head of the table, but food was the last thing on my mind. And yes, contrary to all beliefs, we do eat. It's not a necessity, but it gives me pleasure. It reminds me that I was once human.

Margaret served us dinner and at my command she prepared two glasses. Of course, she understood my discrete sign and while Sarah wasn't looking, she poured wine in hers and blood in mine.

Right after that I sent her home, eager to have more alone time with Sarah.

We started serving dinner, but after only a few bites the air in the room changed and a wave of heat took over my body.

My eyes were looked at her with such desire that I could feel her vibrate across the room.

The unmistakable smell of her arousal was driving my senses crazy. The way she was pressing her thighs together made me let out a long growl "Fuck, Sarah!".

I finished the glass and gathered all my strength for what I had next in mind.

"Come, please!" I spoke clearing the table in front of me then pushing my chair back.

In just a few moments from my calling, she was here and in one swift move, I pulled the table next to me, making her get on the counter.

My hands were now resting on her knees, allowing me to have a few moments to regain my composure.

I took a deep breath and started exploring her warm skin hidden away under her dress. At the same time, trying to keep my cravings a little in control, which was next to impossible to achieve.

I pulled her on top of me in my desire to reach her lips, but by doing that her sensitive flesh collided with my eagerness making me lose focus for a second. I was barely able to guide my lips to explore that sensuous area between her neck and her shoulders while I was ready to lose all restraint.

I stopped just in time, but I couldn't move for a few minutes since my senses were pretty much alerted. The fact that her heavy breathing was making her move just a little against my crotch didn't help either. So, my hand remained tangled in her hair while my senses were soothed by her perfume.

"Wear panties next time, I can hardly contain myself," I muttered a little annoyed at what she was doing to me. No one in all my existence has ever had such power over me. Not having full control only urges me to prove to her that she's not leading this game, *I am.*

I needed her to realize that this connection is real, but at the same time I didn't want to push her into a decision that could change her life. *A decision that I know would be wrong from the start.*

"Sarah. What are you doing here?" I whispered on her lips imagining how it would be to feel them against mine.

"I... I came for the contract," *lies*!

"I must warn you that I don't appreciate being lied to. **The truth, Sarah!** Why are you here?" I needed to hear her say it.

"For the gallery... The contract!" more lies and that cut deep into my soul.

I needed to end this, so, against my will, I placed her back on her feet and helped her rearrange her dress "Very well!"

I had to put distance between us. I stepped away from her, walking towards the other end of the room "The contract! You can inform your boss that you've got yourself a new client. After all, I can't deny you anything you want."

"All transactions will be done by email so that we don't have to physically meet. Let me walk you to the door, I just remembered that I have a business meeting that I can't revoke." This time I was the one lying, but the conjuncture required me to do so.

I walked her to the door, knowing that in just a few seconds I'll let her go.

"It was the right choice, Sarah!" I somehow managed to say, looking into her deep eyes whilst trying to convince even myself of these words.

I knew it was the truth and while shutting the door behind her, I hoped that this would finally shut her out of my life, at least our direct encounters.

I just needed to find a way to do this, now that I had unwillingly let her ***sneak so deep into my soul***.

Miserable days

Sarah

I reached my apartment feeling a completely different person. I was weak. Even though I returned with a victory, I personally felt defeated.

I had lied! I lied because I was afraid of what he really meant to me. I felt like a leaf facing a storm and I got scared, even though now I could never stand under a clear sky again.

Without realizing, my face filled with tears mourning my mistake like the loss of what used to be my life. In fact, I had just lost *what my life could have been.*

I knew exactly what I should do right now. I took off my clothes and got into my bed. I couldn't bear to step into the shower, knowing that it would wash away his touch from my body instantly. I wanted the feel of him to last until at least the morning, since this may probably have been our last encounter.

I closed my eyes, eager to continue what remained unfinished in the dining room. After twisting and tossing, sleep finally came, but the dream that I desired so badly did not come to me. The morning light touched my face, shattering my hopes of seeing him in my sheets that night.

The big day arrived. The day in which I get to savor my sweet success.

Scanning the dressing room, I decided to dress to kill. A white dress shirt, a black molded skirt, and some high fashion snakeskin stilettos were my options for this day.

The apartment door was almost screaming at me to get out and hit the office, so with big steps I rushed down the stairs, got a cab and arrived at work.

Funny how the entrance door seemed to shine brighter today and the big black silvery letters that stood proud in the sunlight were so much more elegant than before. "Timeless Gallery"- this is where I finally found a place of my own.

I entered the workplace and all eyes were fixated on me. Great! What's going on today?!

"Yesterday, you left without an explanation!" Karla's angry voice echoed in the room, drawing even more attention on me.

"I had a really good reason for it," I replied, feeling so proud of myself, but also impatient to give her the news.

Her forehead frowned, unsatisfied with my evasive answer. Oh... She's in for a shock!

"I closed the deal!" I said proudly, unable to wipe the smile of satisfaction off my face. Knowing that I accomplished something so difficult does give me the sense of fulfillment, even though my heart tells me it was a mistake.

"He won't sell anything yet, but he'll make all purchases through us!"

"I hope you're not joking about this!" Karla's voice was trembling, almost unable to believe that it's true.

"I would never joke with something like this. I have actually pulled it off. Now I have to start finding unique artifacts for him."

"And make me some money!" My boss smirked, finally relieved that she got what she desired.

"Where's Jewel?" I ironically asked, looking around the gallery.

"Sapphire was supposed to come in today, but she's not answering her phone. She must be one of those bimbos that just show up to see what the job is about, then move to the next one."

Such a pity, she was beginning to grow on me. Not!

At least I don't have to see her smug face any longer, although it would have been nice to have someone else bringing me coffee for a change.

"See that corner? I'm going to build a glass wall there so that you can have your own office!" She pointed towards a space right next to her own.

"That would be great!" I managed to say, a little overwhelmed by my colleague's looks.

"I'm taking you all out tonight to celebrate!" she pointed at me as if I was her newly discovered treasure.

Things were happening with such speed. People came in just a few hours to measure the space for the office. Karla was ordering a desk from a stylish antique shop, not to mention the attention that the other art dealers were showing me. Most of them never exchanged a word with me until now. I felt like I just won the lottery. The Damien Arion lottery to be precise. My worry was... *Had I just lost the grand prize?*

Later that day I sent him the contract. He made sure I got it back signed in less than an hour, but not a single word more besides the standard attachment file. A small gap formed in my stomach, seeing the formal email, so impersonal given what we shared was so special.

"My little moneymaker," Karla exclaimed while printing the scanned contract. I had managed to do what no other employee had ever achieved.

The day passed and before closing time my boss made sure that no one missed the small 'out of the office' party.

Soon we all headed to a pub two streets away from the office. I didn't really feel like celebrating, but I'm sure that she wouldn't take no for an answer and that my colleagues won't be very pleased if I'd made them skip the free drinks.

Funny how people only notice you after you bring them even the smallest benefit.

I was somewhat disgusted with them. But more importantly, I was disgusted with me. None of the people that we're celebrating my success tonight were my friends. I could even see the envy in some of their eyes, unaware of the sacrifice I just made.

It felt like I was suffocating. I asked myself if this is what I really wanted to become. A dull, insatiable worker forever controlled by a greedy employer, putting my happiness aside for my career.

I kept thinking of a million excuses and people to blame, but the truth was that I was the one responsible. It was my decision and no one else's.

Overwhelmed by the events, I decided to call my one and only real friend. Even though she may not understand what I'm experiencing, she's the only one that truly stands by me for *me*.

"Lala-" I barely spoke on the phone.

"Hun, are you ok? You sound like shit!"

"Where are you?" I asked, hoping she's not working.

"At work, I took a colleague's shift. Her daughter is performing in the school band. Why? What's wrong?"

"Nothing... Too many drinks. I actually called you to come by and celebrate my promotion." I lied because I knew if I told her the truth, she'd come by in a second and that would jeopardize her job.

"You got the promotion?! Why didn't you tell me earlier??? I'm coming down!"

"There's no need to, it's boring anyway. I was thinking about doing something fun with you. How about we go out this weekend?"

"I'm working this weekend, but we'll go next and I know just the place!"

Lala! -a voice echoed in the phone's speaker.

"Go! We'll talk tomorrow!" I rushed her, knowing that she's probably has something else to do.

"Love you!" She quickly added, before hanging up.

"Love you too, crazy!" I smiled, a little surprised at how just a short conversation with her can make me feel so much better.

"Boyfriend?" Karla asked, sneaking up on me.

"No... Best friend."

"Ahhh. Even worse! You can always change the boyfriends. The BF is the one that you're stuck with for life." Karla cheerfully chuckled, trying to be funny.

"I'm getting you a car, by the way."

What?! And she couldn't have started with that?

"A company car at your disposal so that you can go on your antique hunts without being forced to look for a cab."

"I forgot to look at your file. Do you have a license, or do you have to take classes?"

"I got my license when I was 16 back home. But I have never driven since I came here."

"Then I think it's time to get behind the wheel. You'll have quite enough scavenging hunts to make to find pieces for Mr. Arion's collection. The more he buys, the more we make."

I swear this woman is turning into a small grinch with each word she speaks. I literally felt disgusted by the way she was rubbing her hands together, probably dreaming of herself covered in Damien's money.

I suddenly felt nauseous and the fake laughs of the people surrounding me were pounding in my ears, making my loathing for them grow to unbearable proportions.

I knew that Karla wasn't going to let me leave no matter what reason I'd invent. I remained with my colleagues for a few more hours, smiling and trying to fit into a world I once thought I deserved to belong in.

After the drinks stop rolling and the music was losing its volume, I eventually made it back to my apartment. It had never seemed so empty before. *My life never felt empty before.*

Damien managed to alter my whole existence in just two days and as my inner void increased, my body begins to ache for his touch.

I climbed into bed and uselessly hoped I could feel him again, but the minutes of waiting turned into hours and the hours into *miserable days.*

No desert

More than a week passed and I robotically continued going to work and returning home every day.

Lala was really busy with her job, so we only managed to talk on the phone. She sensed something was wrong, but couldn't tell exactly just what my problem was. She made a few idle threats that she would leave the bar and come directly to my place, but did not carry them out.

During the last week I did manage to sell all Mrs. Ullman's paintings for a more than a decent amount. I even made an acquisition for Damien. It was an antique chest, engraved with Celtic symbols, dated somewhere in the late 15th century, which I hope he liked. He didn't answer any of my calls or emails, just made the deposit in the gallery account and a courier delivered the artifact to his apartment. Easy money into Karla's pockets and *more than a few rolled tears down my cheeks.*

I wasn't comfortable doing this. Sure, finding *treasures* for him was a fun task, but not being able to share his excitement, wasn't. I don't even know if he even opened the wooden packing crate it was sent in.

The more I analyzed things, the more restless I became. His silence drove me to my breaking point, so on Friday I got into my brand new company car and drove directly to his apartment.

On my arrival the doorman tried to stop me, but I didn't take no for an answer. I convinced him to let me take the elevator that would lead me to Damien's door.

I didn't have an exact plan at the time. Maybe I could ask him about the recent acquisition, or I could make something up. One thing I knew was that I needed to see him.

I rang the bell and after a few minutes Margaret opened the door with a weird smirk on her face.

"Hello!" I spoke first, not letting her intimidate me with her attitude.

"Hello! Mr. Arion is out!" she rushed to say.

"I'll wait!".... Oh, I'm not letting this old hag close the door on me.

"Mr. Arion is in Rome. He left a few days ago accompanied by Ms. Ember. I'm afraid it will be a while until he returns" - the bitch spoke as if she knew what this news meant to me.

"I understand, thank you," I answered with an almost dejected voice, then headed towards the elevator.

At this point, I couldn't tell if my heart quit beating or the whole world just stopped functioning. Even though I knew that he spends his time surrounded by different ladies, being aware he is with someone else right now was tearing my soul apart.

I'm not sure how I ended up back to my apartment, but as if she heard my door closing, Lala called me the second I entered. I could no longer hold back my tears and my trembling voice led to her being sat on my kitchen chair twenty minutes later.

"I knew you've been hiding something from me. I just thought you were overwhelmed from your promotion, now I clearly realize that's not the case, so spit it out! Is this about Damien?"

Ugh. I wish she didn't know me so well.

"What happened at his place?!" she asked, shifting her eyebrows as if she was trying to think of some options.

"Nothing. He just accepted my proposal of working together."

" And..." she left me to complete the blanks.

"And nothing. We had dinner. That's it!" I don't think that vampires or soul connection would make much sense to her at this moment in time.

"You had dinner with Damien and you say it like it's nothing?! Him saying *hi* to you is something. Dinner is at a whole different level! It's like eating the cherry on top."

"There was no cherry, we didn't have dessert." I ironically answered in the hope that maybe she'll shut up and stop trying to decipher what happened.

"Were you the desert?... Oh, on second thoughts, I bet he'd be a great desert." Lala winked at me as if I didn't already understand what she was implying.

"*No dessert*! Period!" I snapped, bursting into tears as I remembered my choice.

"Hey! It's ok, I didn't mean to make you sad. What's wrong babe? You never cry." Lala wrapped her arms around me, but this time I didn't try to slip away from her embrace. She was the closest thing to family and I needed that comfort right now.

"Sarah, I can't help you if you won't tell me what's wrong, but I understand if you don't want to talk about it."

"I-"

"You can't right now. I understand," she cut me off from completing my sentence.

"I'll make us some coffee. Do you need to go to work today?" She asked filling the water tank then placing it back into the coffee machine.

"I'll just tell Karla that I'm doing some field research. I just can't deal with her today."

"Oh. You wouldn't be lying because we'll do some field research... At the mall. There's no way we're staying here and have you moping around all day."

Ok, now I'm sorry I called her.

"Don't make that face at me. We're drinking our coffee and then you're going to change out of that clearly uncomfortable dress because I'm planning to shop your ass out all day."

"Do I look like I am in a shopping mood?"

"Yes! You look like you're in desperate need of a good shopping session. Today you'll learn the healing effects of silk, cashmere and quality lingerie."

"Don't you have something better to do, like going back to work for example?"

"I've been working like crazy for the last two weeks covering everyone's shifts and throwing in some more of my own. So, if I want an extended weekend then I think I'm entitled to one." Lala was proclaiming her rights just as if she just escaped from slavery.

"I'm sure that you don't want me to stay with you on the couch all day asking you millions of questions about what happened. So, come on and let's get you changed."

I growled, but I just didn't have the energy to fight with her today. The next thing I knew I was in the dressing putting a dress and a pair of sandals on.

"Oh my God! You went to work with Agent Provocateur lingerie on. Who are you, Gates?" Lala couldn't help noticing my choice of lingerie for the day while I was changing my clothes.

I did pay a visit to Damien's apartment in the morning and even though my conscience was telling me to choose H&M, the devil inside pushed me towards a much more seductive choice. How stupid I was! I guess our soul connection didn't get the "*I'm fucking another girl in Rome,*" memo.

I gasped, hurt and irritated at the same time, cursing that moment my eyes meet his. Of all the people out here, I had to find myself one with fangs.

"Come on already, before the mall closes." Lala dragged me from the room, through the exit door.

"The mall's going to be open for another 7 hours." I muttered, knowing that she plans on spending each one of those shopping for who knows what.

"See what I'm saying? We're on a tight time frame here. Hurry up!"

If Damien won't suck the blood out of me then Lala will suck the life out of me for sure.

***

"1....2....3....4....5 This is the fifth shoe store we entered for the last half hour. You keep looking at sandals even though it's almost fall out there."

"They are on sale. I can't buy things that aren't on sale".

"I'll lend you some money, I'll even pay for them myself, just please pick something and let's move on," I desperately pleaded, tired of looking at shoe boxes.

"It's not about the money. It's about the principle. Why pay $100 on shoes, if you can get them a few months later for $30. At the rate I shop in, I'll probably get to wear them next season anyway. Plus, I only buy styles that I'm sure will be trendy the following year too."

"I think you may have missed your calling with the waitress job. You would be more suited as a dressing adviser."

"Well, you could pay me for my advice. Be my first client at the beginning of my new career. With the money you're making these days, you can afford me. Just think about it. I'll be by your side 24/7."

"I'll pass, thank you. Seeing you a day a week is enough. Besides, I'm not sure that my boss would like you to come to work with me every day."

"Yeah... That bitch could use some counseling for herself. Just because she spent two grand on an outfit doesn't mean she can go anywhere in it. You need to dress for the office, not like you're just about to collect your Oscar."

"You hate her more than I do." I laughed, amused by Lala's facial expression every time she mentions my boss.

"Aaaaa. Cosmetics 70% off!!!" - she was already searching the shelves before I even got the chance to enter the store. Just great!

30 stores and 8 shopping bags later, I felt like my feet were about to explode.

"I can't. I give up! I need food, water, alcohol. That's it! I need large amounts of alcohol!"

"You read my mind, Sarah. I need to take my new dress out on a date. What would you say if we went out? If I remember, last week you did promise me a little celebration party."

"I'm not sure if it's because I'm extremely tired, or because I'm one step away from having a nervous breakdown, but it actually sounds really good."

"It's settled then and I know just the place. I always wanted to check the club on the 9th Street out."

"I can't believe that there's a club you haven't went to yet." Lala's got a little club addiction and as a curious young child, she needs to check every single one out.

"I'm not sure how I missed this one. Maybe because it's a little more hidden from the outside view. But who cares? Tonight we're going to *The Count!*"

Joseph

The Count, words that resonated in my mind, touching a recent wound and bringing drops of sweat on my forehead. I was hoping this was exactly what it sounded like, even though the chances that a vampire club would be called The Count were slim to none.

I'm not sure what I was thinking. He wasn't going to be there. Even though I knew that he had found himself another distraction, something was making me want to be near his kind. Maybe because they had started to fascinate me, or maybe just because I was involuntarily trying to replace a void that was now slowly consuming me.

"Hey! You're driving me crazy! You haven't spoken a word for the last twenty minutes." Lala noticed my silence and was making a final attempt to get me back into the real world.

"I was just thinking about what I should wear tonight."

"No, you were thinking of Damien. It's ok, I understand. I would be thinking nonstop about him too if I'd spent more than 5 minutes in the same room with the man."

"Let's go home and change. I don't like where this is going," I muttered, annoyed that sometimes she knows me all too well.

She didn't oppose my idea, mostly because she needed to try on everything she had just bought at least a couple of times.

Soon my apartment looked like a disaster. Shopping bags and clothes all over the place. The devastation was made worse as Lala decided she needed to borrow an outfit for tonight from my dressing room. Apparently, she's no longer taking her dress out, she's taking my clothes out on a date instead.

As I laid on the bed, waiting for her to finish searching my dressing room and finally deciding on an outfit. I must have fallen asleep because the next thing I knew it was dark outside. The fatigue from all the sleepless nights just got to me. But why didn't Lala wake me up?

I made my way to the living room and I couldn't help notice that everything was back in it's place and the disaster from early was replaced by my usual tidy house.

Lala was on the couch, watching TV and to my stupefaction dinner and what seemed to be a vodka shot were waiting for me on the table.

"Ahhh. You're up!"

"Yeah. Why didn't you wake me up earlier?"

"I got your back. Dinner is set and I found our outfits for tonight," she smiled, pointing at two hangers that she managed to pin on the bookshelf.

"And this?!" I looked at the shot of vodka.

"So you get your appetite. Would you prefer the whole bottle? That can be fixed too. Just say the word."

I took a deep breath, trying to keep my strength for later "Let's eat then."

She had prepared a spicy chicken dish that was quite delicious. It came as a shock because last time she cooked my neighbors almost had to call the fire department.

Even though I loved the food, I couldn't eat too much. The knot in my stomach was still there, reminding me that no mistake goes unpunished.

"Do you like these?" Lala was pointing towards the leather tights and a peach corset that was on one of the hangers.

I knew that it was my outfit since the other had the shortest skirt I owned and a small sequins bustier that I usually wear beneath a see-through shirt.

"Isn't yours a little revealing?" I questioned her choice because it left so little skin to be discovered.

"Hey, if I see something I like, I want to be sure I'm taking it home."

" It?"

"Yes, it, as in what's in the pants," she chuckled, winking suggestively at me.

"What about *Class and sass?*" those were the words she used when she was giving me advice about my gala outfit.

"That was for you. Tonight, I'm sticking only with the sass part because my bed's been empty for the last couple of weeks and I urgently need to change that."

"You need to get your head checked."

"Then let's hope I find myself a shrink" this girl had a line for everything. Going against her was useless. This was one of the things that we both shared, a profound ambition for having things our way. And right now, this morning's news was wrecking my plans, even though for the first time I didn't know exactly what those were.

"Get ready! I'll do your hair and you can do mine," she ran to the bedroom and returned with a hair straightener and a bag full of hairpins.

We clowned around for a while and after one and a half hours of preparations, we were finally ready. Well, I was ready in 15 minutes, the rest of the time I had to watch Lala applying and then removing her makeup for at least three times.

"Perfect! The Uber will be here in 5. Move your ass!" *Great*! Now she was the one rushing me.

The ride there was in total silence. Lala blabbered something, but the weight on my chest was preventing me to answer. I started to have the same strange sensation as I did when going to the gala, only this time Damien wasn't going to be there.

I must be overreacting. The stress I've been experiencing lately is taking its toll on me and now it's turning my emotions into paranoia.

The entrance was rather hidden, I even imagined that it was one of the underground clubs in which you need a password to get in. I was a little disappointed when the bouncer just examined us from head to toe then signaled us to go inside. No secret code or anything of that kind.

I walked down the stairs while Lala stopped at the door, flirting with the bodyguard. He seemed to be a little uncomfortable, probably because he was still on the job.

"Lala!" I decided to interrupt her so that we could at least find ourselves a table before she goes missing with some mysterious man.

She finally joined me and offered to scan the place for a table while I got us drinks from the bar. Although, I'm starting to think that we'll end up remaining at the bar since the place was packed.

For some reason, I loved it here. The place had a vintage appeal to it, but not perfectly kept. A certain decadence was the proper word to describe it along with the strong mix of expensive perfumes were assaulting my senses, carrying my thoughts to a place that feels like home.

Mrs. Ullman's apartment first came to mind, but then of course, my thoughts carried me to Damien. *I need a drink.*

"Vodka on the rocks, please! Make it double! And a Cosmo!" I called out towards the bartender that was mixing some drinks.

In a few minutes, they were ready and I impatiently watched how he carefully placed them in front of me.

"I'll get that," a voice resonated from behind me, making the barman nod in approval then turning his attention to another customer.

I turned my chair to see who was offering me drinks, not because I had any intention to flirt, but because I was seriously irritated that someone could think that they had the right interrupt my evening.

"There's no need for you to be upset, I just wanted to be friendly. It's pretty rare to see new faces around this place," the man spoke, making the corner of his mouth curl into a smile.

I took a second to analyze him. Piercing brown eyes and a smile that would convince any woman to fall at his feet were definitely making him stand out in a crowd. To say that he looks pleasing on the eye was an understatement, still, he was no Damien. *No one would ever be.*

But what the hell is he talking about? This is a club. You're supposed to see new faces all the time. I guess he couldn't come up with a better line, even though he seemed like a man that didn't lack communication skills.

"I don't do friendly, not tonight." I quickly put my armor on, sensing that this man could only bring trouble and I have had enough of that for a long time.

"I couldn't find a table." Lala snuck up on me, making her way to the bar so that she'd be reunited with her drink as fast as possible.

"Ugh! Why did I choose these heels? My feet are already killing me!" She whined, shifting from one foot to another.

"Let me fix that for you! Please, ladies," a platinum blond man with a very impressive figure took Lala's arm and walked her to a small table near the bar. I followed, taking the drinks, but not before I looked back at the place the mystery man was standing earlier. There was no one there.

"Thank you for finding us a table!" Lala was looking at him as if he was the ultimate superhero.

"Well, I couldn't have you on your feet all night. It would be rude and I always treat my guests with respect," the man spoke in a tone that I recently heard during my encounter with Damien. I must be going out of my mind, every single gesture, object, sound, you name it, reminds me of him. I feel just like one of those obsessed fans right now.

"This is yours?!" my friend could barely find her words.

"Yes, I own this place. Sorry, it was rude of me, I didn't get to introduce myself. Adam, and you are..."

"Laura, but everyone calls me Lala, and this is my friend Sarah."

"Nice to meet you." I muttered a little concerned that my glass was already empty and I just returned from the bar.

"This place is so beautifully designed," she was trying to get under his skin even though I'm not entirely sure it was necessary.

"I decorated it myself. Do you want to see all of it, we do have a more private section?"

"Of course! I have never been on a private tour," *oh, she couldn't even wait to get home.*

"Sarah?!"

"I'm fine thank you. I'll just stay here with my new friend," I answered pointing at the empty vodka glass.

"Ohhh. Time for a refill!"

"It's taken care of." Adam pointed me to the waitress that was heading towards our table with double vodka and another Cosmopolitan. *I'm starting to like this man.*

"I'll be taking that," Lala grabbed her drink then followed Adam over to a staircase that seemed to lead to a lower level.

"Guess it's just me and you now." I was talking to my glass. The first step to insanity.

"You know, it's pretty weird that you talk to yourself. I didn't figure you as such an introvert," the man from earlier occupied Lala's seat, making himself comfortable.

He was dangerous and I could feel it. I didn't care much at the time since my senses started to slowly numb from the vodka.

The truth is I haven't felt so good in a long time. I didn't feel pain anymore and that was the most important thing.

"Allow me to keep, you company, at least until your friend returns. That way you won't be forced to talk with your glass."

"I guess you have a point, but I must warn you, I'm not a great company these days."

"I think I can handle it," he smiled, emptying his glass then signaling the waitress for a refill.

"Joseph" he nodded.

"Sarah" I smiled out of politeness, letting him run most of the conversation.

Two... or six glasses later I was more than just a little dizzy. Trying to forget is pretty tricky when you have managed to numb everything else except your heart.

"You are quite stunning, Sarah," Joseph smirked, letting me see what I believe to be a fang.

My breath shortened and the glass in my hand broke under the pressure of my palm. A gasp escaped from my throat.

As I looked at my hand, I noticed my fingers covered in blood. I must have *cut* myself. I didn't have much time to react as Joseph took my thumb and placed it in his mouth, tasting my red liquid.

I scanned the room for a second and even though the alcohol was starting to hit me hard, I couldn't help but notice that most of the looks were pointed at me.

Then I returned to Joseph. He was now holding my hand in a tight grip, moving my fingers on his lips. I never was afraid of Damien, but this was something else. Joseph's eyes were turning into a fiery red and my chances of getting out of this alive were reducing each second spent here.

Confusion took over me as a strong arm grabbed me from behind. I was yanked off my seat and held in a position that I could hardly breathe in, not to mention move.

In my bed

"Back down," the voice behind me menacingly barked at Joseph, sending jolts of electricity throughout my whole body. It was the voice that I yearned to hear with every drop of my being.

"Damien," I managed to murmur, surrendering myself in his arms... or passing out from the alcohol. *That part is still a blur to me.*

Damien

At first, I thought my senses were betraying me as I drove my car in the back alley. Maybe I thought of her too intensely over the last few days. In my desire to see Sarah has my mind started playing tricks?

I parked the car and quickly found my way to the entrance. The bouncer just nodded, opening the door. I allowed her scent to fully crash on my skin. *Oh, no. I certainly wasn't mistaken.*

She was here. In the only place in the world I didn't expect her to.

For the last week I spent almost all my nights in Adam's bar, numbing my desires in both alcohol and blood. Sarah was making things difficult for me by trying to get in touch. I had to make Margaret chase her away.

Something inside of me broke when I heard her lying about my whereabouts and especially about my company, but it was at my request. I needed her gone for good, without jeopardizing her recent promotion. *In the end, she's the one that chose this.*

My eyes scanned across the room, to find her. I saw her at a small table next to the bar, with no other than Joseph.

He was one of my sublieutenants back in the days when I was craving for power, but his desires were very different. He needed the blood baths and no sovereignty was enough if it wasn't reddened by the blood of the innocents. I couldn't allow that. I needed an ally, not a monster. I decided to let him go, even though he was the one that brought in the greatest results.

Our roads had crossed over the last centuries, always colliding with his need to show his superiority. *Fool!*

As I was making my way through the crowd, I noticed the glass in Sarah's hand was broken. It had caused her several cuts that were now making the table red with her sweet liquid.

This could only mean one thing. She was in immediate danger! All vampire's eyes turned to her at the smell of blood, not to mention the grip that Joseph now had on her hand as he drank the small drops from her fingertips.

I imagined myself pulling his spine out of his body through his throat for such a gesture, but I knew better. He wasn't alone. He had more than a few servants around and a direct confrontation would place Sarah in even more danger.

My blood unwillingly increased its speed. My eyes turned red and my fangs emerged. Instinctively I pressed my body on Sarah's pulling her as close as I could to my chest.

"Back off!" I growled at Joseph, letting him know that she belongs to me. He may not have been alone, but he knew better than to stand against me right now.

He looked back with a pure animalistic gaze. His eyes pure red with drops of Sarah's blood dripping from his lips.

I yanked her off from the seat and somehow managed to drag her out between the hundreds of vampires that had already detected the scent of blood.

I was hardly able to control myself, but the need for me to protect her was much stronger than anything else. I would have fought them all at that point and would probably have won.

There's a wrath buried deep inside of me that some of them can still remember and fear.

I reached the alley and the adrenaline pumping in my veins was forcing my fangs to surface. With fading powers, I threw Sarah on the backseat of my car and slammed the door shut so that I could recover a little from the smell of her blood.

I soon collapsed to my knees, steadying my body on the car's trunk.

"Is that guy ok? Maybe he needs help." A woman soft voice sounded in my ears, but I couldn't turn to see who it is.

"Are you ok? Let's get you up," a familiar hand grabbed my waist and helped me up onto my feet.

"Don't turn," Adam murmured since my fangs weren't fully retracted. The woman that had spoken earlier was probably not one of us.

"Breath, Damien." he tried to help me. My gaze was fixated on the car window, allowing me to see my beautiful Sarah peacefully sleeping on the backseat.

I finally recovered and turned towards Adam and his companion.

"Damien!?" the young lady exclaimed as if she knew me. I don't remember feeding off her and since Adam hadn't let me turn earlier, maybe she just recognized me from a magazine.

"Do I know you?" I muttered, confused and annoyed at the same time.

"Ahh, sorry, my friend Sarah works for you. She's also here tonight," the woman smiled.

"This Sarah?" I asked opening the car door, but also keeping an eye on Adam so that the smell of her blood won't affect him too much.

"Oh my God! What happened to her?!" the woman almost screamed then ran to the car to check on Sarah.

Adam didn't seem too confused about it. He asked me in the

calmest tone possible "Is that her?"

"Yes! I'm starting to believe that the other is her best friend, so move on to the next one," I muttered. I knew how the night would end for the girl if she were to remain with Adam.

"She passed out, probably from the alcohol, but she managed to cut her hand before doing that. Would you mind taking a look at it?" I asked her, hoping that she'll bandage her wound because I wasn't sure if I would be able to do it.

"I'll get a first aid kit from the bar," Adam immediately disappeared down the stairs.

"Were you about to faint from the blood? Is that why you were leaning on the car so as not to fall?... Men...." the woman laughed ironically.

"Why did you leave her alone?" I barked, realizing what could have happened.

"How was I supposed to know that she'll drink her weight in alcohol in half an hour?! She's supposed to be the calculated one," the woman raised her shoulders just like an innocent child.

Adam arrived in seconds with the medical kit and passed it on to her friend so she could give her proper care.

"The girl is going home," I muttered to Adam.

"Your girl is going home. This one stays here. I like her."

"No, Adam! She won't end up as dinner."

"She won't. As I said, I like Lala. She makes me feel... *alive*."

"You've been dead for over a thousand years, now is not the time to feel alive!" I growled, letting my eyes turn red to show him know that I was not fucking around.

"I won't bite her. You have my word, at least not with my fangs out," Adam chuckled.

Even though he had a weird way of saying it, I knew that he meant it. Honor is amongst one of his few virtues left. At least I saved her friend from getting killed... the other part she can figure for herself.

"All done!" she called out from the car. I assumed Lala was her name since that is what Adam called her.

"Let me!" I helped her rearrange Sarah's body on the backseat so that she wouldn't be uncomfortable.

"I'll take her home!" I let them know that it was time to leave.

"Thank you! Please bring her back... severely damaged." Lala giggled winking at me.

"Oh... I like the way you think," Adam whispered in her ear loud enough for me to hear.

"No, no, no! Out of the two of us, you'll end up being the severely damaged one!" Lala chuckled pulling at his shirt and making me almost burst into laughter. I really like her *and I usually don't like anyone.*

"Adam!" I called out.

"I know. I know..." he answered while descending to the club entrance.

I returned to my car and by some miracle managed to drive back home.

She didn't move from the backseat the whole drive, but my main problem was that I couldn't move her either. Not until I manage to still my thirst. The smell of her blood weakened me to my limit. I couldn't risk her safety by getting too close to her in this condition.

After long thought, I decided it was safer to leave her in the car for a couple of minutes while I went straight to my apartment bar and drank the full contents of one of Adam's bottles. The curse of blood was taking its toll, but this time I knew I didn't have a choice. I needed to overcome my animalistic cravings and make sure she is all right.

I returned to the car and took her fragile body in my arms. This was the second time we've been so close. The feeling of completion was overwhelming me and from the way she snuggled her face on my chest, she felt it too.

I entered the apartment and carried her through the lobby. Even though my head was telling me to take her to the guest room, my heart shouted out differently.

A couple of minutes after leaving the backseat of my car, there she was, in the place that she belonged. Sleeping peacefully *in my bed.*

Coffee

Sarah

My head was pounding, as if a speaker had been implanted there overnight and left on full. I managed to open my eyes for just a second but I had to close them again straight away. The glimpse I caught for that brief moment was enough for me to realize that I'm not in my apartment.

Where am I? I started asking myself while my eyelids were trying to open so that I could scan the room.

I tried to remember the previous night. The last thing I recall was having drinks with Joseph. *Oh my God! I hope I didn't sleep with the guy.*

I remained motionless for a few more minutes, trying to recall what happened and a warm thought came to mind *Damien.*

But he couldn't possibly be there. This must have been all in my imagination. My desire to see him again was playing tricks on me.

I needed to find out where I was as soon as possible but when I tried to get out of bed, I realized I was in my underwear.

This is bad. Really, really bad.

I started panicking, scared of where last night's imprudence had led to.

I examined the room I was in. At first to check if the owner was somewhere around. He was not. Then to see what did I got myself into.

The bedroom was more than imposing. A king-size bed upholstered with a dark blue satin material and golden wood ornaments was the central piece. The walls were decorated with heavy Victorian curtains and crystal candlesticks chandeliers.

If I didn't know better, I'd say I was in the room of a king.

I soon noticed a man's shirt and a pair of shorts on the bed, carefully laid down as if they were prepared for me to wear.

Since I couldn't see my own clothes, I decided to put them on. It sure beats walking around a stranger's house in my underwear. The moment that the clothes touched my skin a familiar scent surrounded me. *The feeling of regret was pressing on my soul again.*

It can't be real I said to myself, taking a deep breath and supporting my body on the wall. I was convinced that at this point I had more alcohol than blood running through my veins.

I'm not sure if anxiety, curiosity or the need for a strong coffee pushed me through the bedroom door. When it cracked open, I almost fell on my knees.

I instantly recognized the hallway I was in. It was the same one that led me to the guest room from a week ago.

With rushed steps, I swiftly headed towards the living room but to my disappointment there was no one there.

A faded smell of coffee caught my attention. I decided to follow its aroma through a black wooden door and down another hallway until I reached its source.

My breath stopped the second the door started to open and the most magnificent sight was right there, before my very own eyes.

Apparently fate, or Damien... or both perhaps, had decided to play with my poor little heart since he was standing shirtless next to the espresso machine, reading what seemed to be an instruction manual. I don't think he heard me coming in because he didn't have any reaction and continued looking at a plastic piece that had just came out of the machine.

I didn't disturb him either, wanting to take another second or two to admire the way his defined back muscles moved while he was doing who knows what with that appliance.

Deep inside I must also be a vampire because the only desire I have now is to bite him.

"Sarah, it's not nice to stare!" - his husky voice snapped me from my thoughts.

Stupid, Sarah. He's a vampire. He felt you the second you came in. Great! Now he'll know that I've been drooling over him for the last couple of minutes.

"What are you doing there?" I quickly tried to change the subject.

"Besides the fact that I live here, I'm trying to make some coffee. But this fucking machine stopped without even finishing the first cup." The Prince of Darkness muttered as if he never encountered regular inconveniences like this before.

"Ahhh. Did 'The King' fall off his throne?" *What the fuck was wrong with me.*

"I was trying to make some for you. If you can recall, I don't need coffee," he growled, abandoning his activity and taking a few steps towards me.

Is this a punishment? Some lessons in repentance? If so, then I regret that I have a big mouth that keeps fucking things up every single time. "I'm sorry, I didn't mean to say that".

"What didn't you mean to say?" he whispered on my skin, letting me know that he wasn't referring at my earlier remarque.

"What I just said, about the throne. I guess the alcohol didn't leave my system yet."

"What we're you doing there?" - he cut me off with a menacing voice while every single one of his muscles tensed.

Maybe I'm crazy, but this was the hottest thing I ever witnessed. Instead of backing down like a little deer, I was strangely aroused. Next time he wants to play this game, he better have a shirt on, because he's getting nowhere this way.

"Sarah?!" he muttered again making his eight pack move. Did

this man train throughout all eternity?... I think I might still be a little drunk.

Focus Sarah, focus! Eyes up!

"I went for drinks with my friend. How was I supposed to know the club would be full of vampires? I didn't even know vampires existed until a couple of weeks ago," sometimes my come back lines surprise even me.

"Why didn't you leave when you realized it?"

"It was too late because I was already on my.... my.... sixth glass."

"Sixteenth maybe," he growled again, grinding his teeth.

"I messed up, ok? But what were you doing there anyway? Weren't you supposed to be screwing some model in Rome?"

"Do I sense jealousy again Sarah?" he whispered, placing his thumb on my lower lip.

"Who would have saved you if I was in Rome?" Damien continued, lifting my chin up so I'd be able to look directly in his eyes.

"I like your jealousy. There's a certain darkness in it that I find very attractive."

"I'm not jealous," I muttered, unwilling to give him the satisfaction.

"You are such a bad liar. You clench your fists every time you lie. I know this because you've done it before even if I specifically told you I don't like being lied to! This gets me angry. When I'm angry my mind goes to dark places. Maybe I'll end up punishing you for this behavior! Or maybe you want that?!"

Is that a question, because I'm not sure that the right answer exists? Yeah... I'm definitely still drunk.

"Coffee... You were making me coffee. I really need one right now." I changed the subject again because I knew where this was going and I wasn't prepared to give him an answer just yet.

"I'll have to read that damn manual first. I should have thought twice before buying the most expensive espresso machine that they had. The higher the price, the higher the number of useless functions."

"Let me. Maybe I can fix it." I murmured, walking past him and starting to work on the espresso machine.

I could hear him searching for something in the closets and when I turned, he was pouring himself a glass of wine.

"What time is it?" I asked a little confused because of the lack of exterior windows. It was like all connections with the outside world were cut off...and it felt so good!

"It's noon," he replied, emptying the glass, then taking a seat on a chair behind me.

"Aaa. Done! The water tank wasn't placed correctly and I think it had a safety that prevented it from functioning so" I was so proud of myself... *Girl power*!

"Damien, did you like the chest I bought?"

"Yes, it's exactly what I would have picked."

"Good. I thought you didn't even open the package," I spoke, finally managing to take a sip of coffee.

"I opened it when it came in. It's in the guest room now."

The guest room, such sweet memories.

"Come here!" he ordered in a commanding voice that didn't leave me any room to deny it.

I placed the cup on the counter. My unsteady legs carried me right over to him in just a few seconds.

He didn't say a word, but his index finger rested on my kneecap while he looked straight up at me to see my reaction.

I didn't move, not because I have some extraordinary self-control ability, but mostly because I was almost out of breath waiting for his next move.

"Sarah," he whispered trailing his finger lightly up my inner thigh.

"I don't like to be kept waiting," he smirked, moving his hand up beneath my shorts.

"What are you doing here? This is the last time I'm asking!", he growled.

My first thought was to tell him that he brought me here, but it wasn't the time for a sarcastic reply... besides, I knew better than anyone that I brought myself here.

"I-" my voice was trembling, knowing what this meant.

"*I belong here!*" I finally managed to get that weight off my chest, but I never expected what happened next.

In one second, he lifted me up around his waist and slammed my body on the kitchen wall while his lips crashed against mine. This wasn't a sweet gentle kiss. He was controlling me, claiming me as his, and I was enjoying every last second of it.

Fate waged a hand in this game in which we were the main pawns. That kiss was the bond that was sealing our future.

His tongue hungrily explored my mouth. I could feel his fangs pressing against my lips, making him growl a few times, probably trying to keep them in place.

After a few minutes, he slowed down. This led into a much more sensual pace that managed to heighten the sensitivity of every last possible inch of my body that had previously been numbed from the alcohol.

He stopped, placing his forehead on mine to look into my eyes while his palms cupped my face. "*Good decision, Sarah,*" he whispered over my lips, trying to catch his breath.

If I had any doubt about my destiny, it was just shattered by this amazing man standing right here in front of me, *Damien Arion*.

Darkness

"Have dinner with me tonight," Damien murmured, slowly placing me back on the ground, while still holding my body close to him, probably sensing that my feet still couldn't fully support my weight just now.

How can I deny him? I'm pretty sure I could never deny him of anything again, or that I'll even want to. Still, my charming personality decided to surface "Isn't it a little early for dinner, Mr. Arion?"

"You've got quite a mouth on you. I think I'll have to find a way to shut it up," he growled, pulling me back into a kiss and slowly biting my lower lip.

For once the fact that I can't keep my mouth shut actually paid off.

If someone were to tell me on the night of the ball that someday I'd be standing in Damien Arion's kitchen, kissing him, I would laugh in their face. I think Lala would actually faint if she'd known...*Wait...Lala.*

"Damien!" I broke off the kiss and started to panic.

"What's wrong?!" a look of concern passed over his face.

"My friend! I left her in a vampire club. I need to call her." I searched for my phone, but realized that I was wearing Damien's clothes.

"Calm down! She's ok. She's with a friend of mine."

"That Adam guy?! You know him?"

"For a few centuries."

"He's also a vampire?! What if he bites her?!"

"No offense, but judging by last night's events, things would probably evolve the other way around." Damien chuckled, making me realize that the scale was inclined in my friend's position.

"But why aren't you concerned about your own safety? What if I'll bite you?" he whispered seductively, letting one of his fingers travel from the crock of my neck to his shirt's collar, then slowly descending between my cleavage and down over my stomach to the base of my shorts.

Even though my legs were beginning to shake a little, but not by fear, I gathered all my inner strength to answer him "If that was your intention, you would have done it by now."

"Maybe I'm saving you up for later," he whispered, pulling me back in his arms.

"I'm counting on that." I went in for a kiss this time. Since there was a height difference, I had to get much closer, realizing that our flirting was starting to have repercussions in his pants.

He lifted me up onto the kitchen counter and took control of the kiss, pressing his body insanely close to mine. His tongue started twisting and playing against my own while his hands were finding their way beneath my shirt when all of a sudden, a sharp pain flashed through my palm. In my ecstatic state, I forgot about the cuts and clenching my fist had reopening some of them.

In seconds Damien detached from my embrace and desperately searched for his wine glass... *Shit! I don't think that is wine.*

"The hand" he was barely able to breathe. He sipped what was left in the glass, then quickly refilled it.

"I'm sorry!" I immediately ran to the living room, to search for something to change my bandage.

I looked around for a few minutes, but I couldn't find anything around. I decided to cross my fingers and call Margaret.

"She's not in." Damien stepped out of the kitchen, but still keeping a significant distance. "Try the bathroom cabinet," he pointed towards another black wooden door.

I rushed in and finally found a generous supply of medical products. They're probably here for Margaret or for the other ladies that visit Damien. *Ugh! My mind just went there again.* I have to learn to control my jealousy, especially since he knows this is my weak spot.

After a few minutes I managed to change my bandages, throwing the old ones in a trash bag. I made sure to wrap them up really well to be sure that the smell wouldn't bother him.

"Are you ok?" I asked, returning to the kitchen. I noticed that the bottle was empty.

"I'm sorry I couldn't help you with the bandage. I have to adjust a little." He sighs, searching the cabinet and opening another bottle.

"You can go back to the bedroom if you like," he spoke in a much colder tone, turning his back on me and filling up the glass.

I had no intention of listening to him. Especially since I knew why his voice lost its warmth.

"I don't care that its blood," I spoke, leaning my forehead on his back.

"Sarah..."

"I'm not a child. I know you don't survive on air."

Suddenly I heard my phone starting ring, but I couldn't exactly trace the source.

"It's in the living room. You were out of battery so I charged it." Damien spoke while I was already following the sound.

"Lala! Are you ok?!" I had managed to answer my phone before she hung up.

"I was about to ask you the same thing. Considering that I left you with Damien, I knew that if something was broken, he would have fixed it by now!" she giggled in her signature way.

"I see you're functioning at full capacity.

"Not really, every bone in my body hurts, but in the right kind of way."

"I'm not sure if I drank too much, or maybe it's because I haven't drink enough, but I REALLY don't want any details."

"You know I'm not shy. This man kept me awake all night long."

*That's because he's a vampire, Dumdum. ...**And so is Damien...***

"Man?! Did anything else happened?!"

"Like what?!.... Oh... Something did happen... I fell in love with Adam!"

"No, you probably fell in love with his *skills.*"

" Minor details."

"Are you on the phone?!" A voice echoed through the other end.

"Are you still there?" I asked Lala, convinced that it was Adams's voice.

"Why, Sister Mary, are you at your place?" she chuckled, placing the guilt on me.

"I don't think it's the same situation."

"What are you waiting for... Make it the same! I have to go to..."

"Hang up, right now before you put an image in my head that I won't be able to erase, even with the best shrink in town."

I shook my head, already exhausted from this conversation. It's like she's feeding her energy with my own, or with my nerves, I'm not sure at this point. But I would be lying if I didn't admit that despite all her craziness, she's my best friend and I love her.

I entered the kitchen and Damien was in the same position, lost in thought and frowning, probably because I had realized it wasn't wine - but blood.

"I... I need to go home and get changed" I switched the subject to try and distract him from his reflections.

"Stay here. I'll order you a dress for dinner."

"Where are you going to order a dress from in two hours?!" I knew this was NY, but a dress isn't like ordering a pizza.

"I may be a vampire, but to the outside world I'm still Damien Arion. I can get you a whole dress store in an hour. Don't underestimate me!" For a second a flash of empowerment ran through his eyes and I could feel his vampire nature mixing with the human one.

I didn't fight back, at least not this time. Even though a hundred witty answers were flashing through my mind at this moment.

"Can I take a shower?!" I asked, almost biting back my tongue.

"Of course you can, use the one in my room. Get an hours sleep if you want, you need it after last night. I have a few phone calls to make anyway."

"Are you saying I look tired?" I chuckled, unable to keep my mouth this time.

He looked at me with the same arrogance I saw just a couple of seconds ago. I recognized what he was doing right away. He was trying to control me.

"I offered you my bed *to sleep in.*" His hand cupped my face while his thumb started stroking my lips, slowly lifting my chin up so that I can look him straight in the eyes.

The corner of his mouth curved into a devilish smirk as he approached my lips, whispering in my mouth "This is a one-time offer because *I never sleep.*" His thumb gently parted my lips, then retreated, making room for his tongue to sneak in and steal a kiss, leaving me defenseless in front of him.

He has a passion that sets me on fire. The thought that a person as calculating as Damien can burn so intensely on me pushes my mind into its darkest corners, making me crave a world surrounded by darkness... *His darkness.*

Show no weakness!

I lost myself between his silk sheets for an hour or so, relaxing my body from what had been a short, but wild night. Damien was right, I needed this. I just didn't realize how much until my head hit the pillow and my eyes closed so that I could fully enjoy the feeling of *home*.

When I finally woke up, I started searching the room for my bag, in the hope that Lala managed to throw in some makeup products before I left. Even though his bathroom had everything I could possibly need, I highly doubt that I could stumble on a makeup palette while searching the drawers.

It seems I do have some good luck today. I was able to find a mascara and a lipstick in my purse. That should do.

I arranged my hair up and put a little makeup on. I then went in search of Damien. I felt bad in a way that I had chased him out of his own bedroom, but I would have no problem sharing, if he would only ask... *Who am I kidding? I would have been terrified if he would have asked, but still* **willing to share.**

I reached the living room, but he wasn't there. I sat down on the sofa admiring his portrait again. I keep thinking about his former life, the places he must have seen, the challenges he must have faced.

"Your dress arrived," Damien snuck up on me and made me gasp at this unexpected appearance.

"You startled me!" I admitted as he took a place next to me on the sofa, making my breath shorten.

He must have changed while I was asleep. If his normal presence gave me trouble focusing, now I couldn't do anything but stare and wonder to myself how on this earth I managed to end up with a man like this.

His jet black hair was carefully slicked back, but a small strand had detached and was falling over his deep green eyes.

He smiled, knowing that I was studying him. I couldn't help myself from staring at the small dimple that was forming in his cheek from his gesture.

My eyes descended, yearning to touch the ink that was peeking from under his collar, creating a storm inside of me and an ache to find myself in his arms. My greedy eyes were not satisfied and needed to also feast on the image of the black dress shirt wrapping his torso flawlessly, letting every muscle show its defined shape under the material.

I managed to stop before I reached other places that would definitely change the dynamic of our evening.

"What are you thinking of?" Damien asked me in a playful tone as if he was reading my mind. *I am so busted!*

"Nothing, in particular, I guess I didn't fully recover from last night."

"What did I say earlier?" he asked with annoyance, placing his hand on my waist and then pulling my body on his lap.

I instantly lost my breath and even though I kept trying to recall what he was talking about, it was useless. My mind turned into a blank page where an imaginary pen was writing only his name.

"I'm not sure what you're referring to," I manage to mutter in an annoyed tone. *Show no weakness!*

He smiled, but this wasn't an innocent one. The devil inside was trying to emerge and I'm not sure if the anxious state he was created inside me was because I was scared, or because I was eager to meet his other side.

"I told you not to lie to me," this time his tone was more imposing and his hand found its way under my shirt, slowly exploring my legs.

"Were you thinking about this?" he smirked, stopping his hand as it reached the base of my left breast, then slowly tilting his head and grazing my lower lip with his teeth.

This was beyond sensual and the small flickers of pain that were dancing on my lip were only making me crave for more.

"Dinner," my stupid mouth decided to speak for itself, ignoring the rest of my body's needs.

"You must be hungry." Damien lifted me to my feet "Go change" he glanced at a white box that was sitting on the glass living room table.

I was a little anxious to see the dress. Even though I had two previous relationships, no man has ever bought me a piece of clothing before. Maybe the fact that they were both assholes had something to do with it. I'm not sure why, probably because this was the kind of gesture I saw only in movies, but his presence was making me special.

I unwrapped this beautiful white box the second I reached the bathroom and even though I knew I was going to like his choice, what I found overcame my expectations.

A beautiful lace black dress decorated with silver beads and sequins, probably hand made. There wasn't anything tacky about it, on the contrary, it had a vintage look, intertwined, with the latest catwalk designs.

I put it on and the generous cleavage made me smile, realizing that it was the advantage I had in front of Damien for the evening. No man or vampire could ever resist a beautifully packed gift. *Did I mention that modesty isn't my strong point?*

"I'm ready!" I seductively whispered, stepping out of the bathroom and enjoying the hungry look on his face while his eyes were roamed over my body completely.

"Come!" he instructed, and even though I hate being ordered, his tone made me obey.

And then I realized. *He's the only one that will ever command me.*

He opened the front door and waited for me to leave and we then made our way to his car.

His taste in antiques did not apply to cars since he owns the latest Maserati model. A man of power and speed.

The ride was relatively short and I didn't get too much time to admire his skills behind the wheel. Even though I'm not a great driver myself, I always had a thing for men driving muscle cars. Call it *my guilty pleasure.* Maybe it has to do with the adrenaline, and if so, I must be in luck, because the adrenaline rush was definitely a joy that Damien isn't going to deprive me of.

The car stopped on a dark alley, similar to the one The Count is located in.

Damien threw me another one of his signature devilish smiles, then got out of the car and came around to open my door.

He didn't lack manners, that's for sure. He offered me his hand and led me towards a mahogany wooden door. The second we were in front of it, it cracked open and a beautiful redhead signaled us in.

"Good evening! Private booth?" the woman asked.

"Yes!", Damien muttered, gave my hand a reassuring squeeze, then placed me in front of himself putting his other arm around my waist.

We walked down a long dark hall with dim red lighting. It actually reminded me of the dungeons I saw drawn in books, but this place had a certain sensuality to it.

We finally reached a big saloon with possibly over 30 dinner tables. I managed to study the people present and based on my assumptions most of them were vampires, but a few among them were *normal people.*

The instant we entered the room all eyes were on us. I'm not sure how, but entering on Damien's arm was seeding a feeling of pride deep inside of me

He didn't say a word, just walked me to a private booth in the corner of the room. But as we passed between tables, I noticed how the other vampires were bowing their heads in his presence, like he was some kind of royalty.

He carefully made room for me to slide onto the leather couch, then occupied the place right next to me.

My eyes started admiring the room, studying the large chandeliers that looked over the chamber, throwing a shadowy light on the wooden tables.

Every person attending was elegantly dressed, but most of their clothes had a new vintage style, like the past and the present were combining in a flawless manner.

"What is this place?" I asked, unable to control my curiosity as a beautiful woman started singing a 20's song.

"I like to come here to relax. It's like a free zone. Usually, normal people don't come here unless accompanied by one of our own, but there are some exceptions."

"I like it. I feel like I belong here... *In this world.*"

"Sarah, I wish so badly that you would..."

"The menu," a voice interrupted him and postponed this subject for another time.

"We'll have a bottle of Terrantez Madeira and we'll decide on diner shortly" Damien ordered, opening the menu.

"You don't have to order wine. I saw the glasses on the other tables. I know they have..."

"You can say it, Sarah. They have blood".

I took a deep breath trying to figure a way not to mess things up this time. I knew that he was disturbed earlier in the kitchen when I found out what was in his glass. "Yes, blood. I think you'd want that instead of wine."

"Actually, this is the only wine I like. Probably because it's one of the oldest wines in the world that's still drinkable," he smiled, shifting his body towards me.

A sudden sadness came over his face and I felt that it was getting hard for him to speak. "I don't want the blood. I need it. Especially when I'm around you."

My eyes widened, realizing the trouble he must go through just to stay with me in the same room.

"I need the blood to control my thirst. I usually don't have that problem, but you... You're special. Your blood is very different," he took a deep breath, searching my eyes to see if I'm still with him.

"Order it, please!" I rushed to speak, unable to live with the thought that I was putting him through such torment.

"Are you sure? I don't want you to feel uncomfortable."

"Seeing that I provoke your pain makes me uncomfortable," I answered, relieved that the waitress was arriving.

"Get me a glass from one of Adam's bottles," he commanded the second she filled our wine glasses.

His lips curved into a smile, grabbing my waist to get even closer to him while his hand made room between the sequins of my dress and on to the thin lace that was covering my skin.

His glass clinked on mine setting the tone for what was about to come "*For a very promising night.*"

Tune of victory

We were served dinner. I know he was only eating so I wouldn't feel uncomfortable. I also think this was giving him a lost feeling of normality, when in fact, *nothing will ever be normal again.*

He was still sipping from his glass, maybe letting his thoughts stray a little, but his fire was still there. He was making my body subdue to his mere presence and my mind to wander to the nights he visited my room.

His hand found mine and started to play with my fingers while he kept looking at the bandage that covered my cut.

"You said my blood is special. How's that?" I finally broke the silence that set between us, eager to find out what he meant.

"This isn't the right place to talk about it. As private as it looks, eyes will always be looking at us," he smiled placing his arm around me and shifting my body a little so I could see the whole room.

"Look at them, they all fear and respect me, but this is nothing compared to how things used to be. I was in a dark place, a big part of me still remained there. My thirst for control still surfaces from time to time, especially around you," he whispered, making every cell in my entire body ignite.

In a way, I loved that about him, the power he had over me, but my tongue always outpaced my mind. "You'll never control me." I immediately responded, raising up a storm.

"In less than one week, you'll be begging me to do it!" he muttered, rearranging the collar of his shirt, then emptying his cup.

I knew I had awoken a monster, but who said I don't like to live dangerously?

"I guess we should be leaving then. Time is running out." I always liked to play with my cards on the table, it gives me more satisfaction when winning. But, I'm not sure about this game, I guess we'll have to wait and see in the morning.

He didn't say a word, but his hand reached my knee, then went up on the outside of my thigh until it grabbed my posterior with a strong grip. I gasped, in a lame attempt to get rid of the knot that was now bothering me. "Just imagine if this piece of material wasn't in the way," he grinned, moving his hand on my body until he reached my chin and lifted my head so I could look directly at him.

"Check, now!" he muttered to the waitress that was just approaching our table without losing eye contact with me.

I was more than intimidated but even more determined not to show him my state of spirit.

The waitress returned with the check. As soon as he had taken care of it, he seized my hand and led me out the same way we had come in from.

We reached the car, but as usual, my curiosity got the best of me. I guess some people don't ever grow up and I'm one of them. "Is this the right place to talk? There's no one else here besides us." I needed to know and I'm not sure that I would get answers once we reach the apartment. I seductively smiled, letting him in on my future intentions.

"You'll get answers when we get there and you'll also be able to decide what to do with them," he answered with a sad tone that resonated in my mind all the way back.

Contrary to my expectations he didn't sweep me off my feet and break the bedroom door down as I had secretly wanted. On the contrary, Damien kept a certain distance and once we reached his apartment asked me to take a seat on the leather couch.

His silence started to send a cold chill racing down my back. Seeing the calculated manner in which he was opening a fresh bottle of blood and filling his glass allowed fear to settle in.

"Do you know what an Amplifier is?" He finally asked after a few minutes of tormenting stillness.

"Like something that intensifies stuff?"

"Yes, but not stuff... Powers. You see, you're special."

"Mrs. Ullmann mentioned something when I was at her apartment."

"Ahhh. Natalia... Not a fan of mine, but I guess she already let you in on it."

" She was just concerned about me....and the path I'll choose."

"What did she say to you?"

"Only that I'm special and that if I choose to be like a witch or a vampire, my powers would be greater than usual."

"That's it?"

"Yeah, that sums it up."

"What she said... It's true... But that's not all," he murmured in a quiet voice.

"Your blood, if consumed by a vampire, also enhances his powers." His deep green eyes were staring into mine, searching for a reaction, but my mind was just putting two and two together... Him...Joseph... The wound on my hand.

"You can't go back to your apartment... Or your former life... Joseph knows now what you are. He tasted it in your blood that night."

"What do you mean?! My life! My job!"

"He'll come after you if you're not under my protection and I can't have that!"

"So, what will happen?"

"I was thinking you could stay with me. I'll talk to your boss to arrange that you can work from here. Maybe you'll go out after dark, so I can keep an eye on you. We'll figure something out."

"You mean I'm a *prisoner*?!"

"Is that how you feel?"

"No, I didn't mean to say that... I'm just a little overwhelmed. "

"It's ok."

"That's the reason why you have trouble around me?"

"Yes... The fact that you're my... half and an amplifier complicates things a lot. I used to think that this *soul connection* was nothing more than a myth... That was until I felt you that night. I was aware for a while of that possibility, even since my soul kept visiting you. But I was starting to think that maybe it was a trick played by my bored mind."

"Does it hurt? Being around me?" I asked, terrified of what his answer might be.

"I don't care if it hurts. I'm much more concerned about not harming you. I haven't had trouble with self-control in more than 300 years, but sometimes when I'm around you, I seem to lose it."

"I'm starting to learn to contain it. I think I have most of it figured out, but I need to make sure it stays that way."

"So, this is it?! The life I used to know is over?!" My sight was starting to blur from the tears forming in my eyes.

"I could kill him, but he has a lot of devotees and there's no doubt that some of them already know about this. Others will only come in his place. At least I know his game... all of his moves."

"This means that I'm putting you at risk."

"I fought battles, even wars alone. I led armies and defeated kings. He knows better than to come after me. He may be desperate, but not stupid. As long as you're with me, you're safe."

"I want you to realize that you feeling like a prisoner... That's the last thing I want."

"I didn't mean that... I was confused... Still am."

"I understand if you want to be alone... You can sleep in my room." He turned his back on me so that he could refill another glass. But I knew that wasn't all. He didn't want me to see the sadness in his eyes.

"I know it's my fault this has happened... But as crazy as it may sound, I don't regret it... It got you back with me... And our cards are finally front up on the table," I murmured standing up from the couch and heading towards him.

I watch him turnaround, a little confused, yet also relieved that I hadn't made a drama out of this. Any other person would, but not me.

Have I gone mad? Maybe so, but I saw this as an opportunity and not a curse. Sure, there were a lot of things we needed to learn about each other. Me staying here will only speed that process up.

Regarding my job... I'm sure that one phone call from Damien would convince my boss to let me work anywhere, even on the Moon.

"This evening has deviated very quickly," I pointed out as I placed my hand over his and clasped it around it.

"You're certainly different," he smiled, placing his glass down and capturing my other hand so he could pull me next to him.

"I guess this time the messenger gets to live," he growled approaching my lips.

"I'm not so sure, the messenger gets stuck with me."

"Fucking perfect!" he sealed his declaration with a kiss.

My hungry mouth quickly parted so it would make room for his tongue. Even if I wanted never to break that kiss, the way his hands clasped on my hips were moving things fast to the next level.

He lifted me up and my legs found their place around his waist while he carried me through the dark hall straight to his bedroom.

Things were falling all around us, but neither of us cared. He placed me on the bed and let his body come on top of me while supporting his own weight.

He started growling, slowly biting my lips in between kisses while his fingers were lifting my dress up, just to take it over my head in the following seconds.

I didn't fall behind and threw his shirt on the floor, letting the sound of it hitting the ground be *my tune of victory.*

I wasn't a regular person... Maybe special... Maybe just insane... But being **his** was a dream that had for far too long been postponed.

I watched him as the tattoos on his body came alive, dancing for my pleasure. Every single breath this man took was making me melt into him. And as his hand grabbed my hair so he could have access to my neckline, my legs wrapped around his waist, closing all distance and feeling the hardness beneath the material of his pants.

His tongue started moving on my neck and the movement of my hips matched its pace. My nails slowly grazed his back, making him *fully* aware of just what he was doing to me.

I could hear him growl with pleasure. All of a sudden, he stopped and pushed me into the mattress so hard that I thought it will leave bruises. It was like he was trying to distance himself and in the next moment I knew why. He looked at me with devil red eyes and fangs fully out in the open.

For a second I stood still, terrified of him for the first time... Because he wasn't my Damien anymore... *The monster took control!*

Next to you

I stayed still and absolutely silent as I watched him storm out of the room. I heard the doors closing behind him.

The recent events kept replaying in my mind. I realized that we had rushed things which probably caused him to lose control. The smell of the blood from my hand combined with the adrenaline and lust was just too much of a push.

I stayed there for what seemed like an hour, not even moving a muscle. I was thinking about what all of this means and what kind of life this could give me. All questions were leading me to the same answer *him.*

Damien was everything to me and all that I wanted. My job, my former existence, nothing else mattered. I just wanted him and all the consequences that might imply.

An unknown power was pushing me to leave the room in search of *my vampire* even though common sense said the opposite.

I abandoned the bedroom and walked through the dimly lit corridor, trying to find the chamber he was in.

I opened every door I encountered, but couldn't find him until I reached one that had recent scratches marking it. I instantly knew this is where he was.

I tried to open it, but it was stuck. I twisted the knob hard and the door parted. I searched for a light switch as I had in all the other rooms, but this one was different. I could sense it, even though it was completely devoid of light and I couldn't see a thing.

"Leave Sarah," his voice broke through the darkness, but instead of sending me away, it drew me further inside.

"No! I came here because *here* is where you are and this is where I want to be. I need to be in this house...in this room, *next to you.*"

"I lost it earlier. I couldn't control myself and put you in danger. You should leave."

"Am I in danger now?" I asked, already knowing the answer.

"No. But you could be in any minute," he murmured, still remaining in a corner of the room where I couldn't clearly see him.

As my eyes slowly adjusted to the darkness, I realized the space was empty. Only stone-cold walls that somehow threw me back in time, into an age that I didn't seem to know, yet strangely felt like home.

He probably comes here to be alone, to isolate himself from the rest of the world, *but he's not alone anymore.*

"I think we rushed things a little... Both of us. But that doesn't mean the night is lost." I used a seductive tone, leaving him in no doubt as to my intentions.

A pair of fangs won't stand in the way of five hundred nights during which I fully expected him to finally claim what's rightfully his.

A cold chill traveled down my body, only to be replaced by the familiar warmth of his presence.

I stood still, feeling his breath on my skin letting it infiltrate into my flesh until I became drugged with *him.*

His lips starting grazing my back, melting instantly all thoughts of resistance my womanly thinking could come up with.

I waited silently, a little impatient for his next move, then his lips finally started traveling my collarbone, I unwillingly gasped, preparing for whatever was to come be next.

"I'm not going to bite you Sarah," he whispered, letting the power of his words hit the moist skin that his lips had just traced and subduing my last drop of free will.

His tongue found the place on my neck where earlier I thought that his fangs will be. At the same time that one of his hands cupped my breast making my dress strap fall off my shoulder.

He growled but didn't repeat the earlier mistake and rush things. On the contrary, he found my lips and we fell into a passionate kiss, while making sure my dress fell to the floor for the second and hopefully, last time this night.

"Don't move," he spoke between kisses, slowly lowering himself to explore new areas of my skin.

Easier said than done because standing still while Damion's mouth was traveling across my body was both pleasure and pain. I felt like a contestant at one of those endurance games and in this rhythm, I was sure to lose.

His lips reached my breasts, but without removing my bra he slowly bit my hardened peaks, then descended on my abdomen, covering every inch of it in kisses... *He could torture me like that for all eternity.*

I was barely breathing at this point, feeling his tongue roaming my skin and the second it pressed on my navel my knee caps almost turned to mush.

"Stand," he growled, pressing his tongue a little harder on the spot that made me so weak earlier. *I'm starting to believe that this is sexual torture.*

I had so little power left in me and he was still at the upper part of my body. This was making me realize that the nights his soul came to my bedroom didn't prepare me for the sensation his flesh on mine can provide.

He started to descend again, placing his hands between my thighs to set them apart and giving my soft flesh a slow bite through my panty's material.

"Damien!" I couldn't help myself, a little scared that I might faint if he'll keep me standing for what comes next.

"Let's take this to the bedroom," he smirked, getting back on his feet and then lifting me up on his waist, moving towards the bedroom.

I was amazed how my weight on his body seemed to be close to none and the way he started kissing me reminded me of one of those movie scenes that everyone dreams to live, but no one actually does.

Well, I do. Damien is about to make *every single one of my dreams come true*. I can feel it.

A small bump made me open my eyes. Damien had just hit the bed frame, probably too focused at the way my nails started to wonder his back.

He placed me on the silk lining slowly, bringing his body on top of mine, uniting our lips again.

I could feel him starting to breathe faster and faster while he was removing my bra. I cupped his face, breaking the kiss for a moment.

"I'm ok," he answered, like almost hearing my unspoken question.

"But you won't be," he growled, grabbing the base of my chest with his hand and covering my rosy tip with his mouth.

I definitely won't be ok after this night.

He started nibbling, then rotating his tongue, forcing my legs to press harder and harder on his waist.

I guess he quickly noticed because one of his hands came down, removing my panties. I could feel him grinning while his fingers found my folds and started massaging my sensitive spot.

I pushed my back deep into the mattress while his mouth descended to my navel, pacing the rotation of his tongue with the of his hand.

My end was so near, I could feel it, but he lifted his head and shook it as a NO..... *Yes, I was now sure, my Damien was torturing me.*

He didn't return to my abdomen but instead placed himself a little lower and his lips found *mine,* pressing my thighs even further apart gaining access to the place he wanted.

His tongue started rotating again against my flesh, making me praise all Gods that brought me here tonight, while he let one of his fingers fill me.

The room was practically spinning. The pulses on my nub combined with the curving of his finger inside were enough to send me into overdrive.

"Come here," I moaned, hoping it will stop him for a while and I won't be lost in less than ten minutes since we reached the bed.

He didn't answer as a second finger found its place, grinding on my walls with movements that were increasing speed, causing the room to be filled with the sounds of my moans. In a few minutes it was game over, my body began to shake as all its energy was leaving it.

I wish he would stop, but his hand replaced his lips, not giving me a chance to rest while he lifted himself on top of me placing his hard member at my entrance.

My eyes widened, locked on his while he was gently pushing himself inside.

I must be out of practice since I hadn't had sex in ages, but I don't think this was a regular size.

I didn't move, steadying my breath while he slowly started to grind, leaving me enough time to get accustomed.

I could sense him pausing a few times, but then quickly regaining his pace. I know that in these moments it's hard for him to keep control, but I need Damien here and not the version he keeps locked inside.

I met him with a kiss, pulling his body even closer to calm him down a little, so that he won't lose it.

Big mistake on my part, because he pinned my hands over my head, and not breaking the kiss, pushed himself harder inside.

It was too much, but somehow, I wanted more. His slow but long movements were making *ME* lose control. Thank God that I'm not the one with fangs because I would have bitten him all over long ago.

Our breaths intertwining was the only thing you could hear in the room. The way he was breaking our kisses just to look in my eyes while he was pushing deeper made the moment even more erotic. He was owning me and I was finally becoming *his*.

I could feel that he was close from the way his grip on my wrists tightened and I couldn't hold my body back anymore from spasming.

I was moaning in his mouth between kisses when he let out a growl, filling me with his heat even before I was done.

"Are you ok?" he asked, looking at my wrists that were a little red from his force.

"Perfect," I reassured him, trying to make sense of what just happened. I can't deny that I was a little shocked by the way our bodies worked together in perfect harmony, but that could only mean one thing. He was really my half.

"You are so beautiful," he smiled, traveling one of his fingers on my swollen lips.

"Are you tired?" he asked, lifting his weight off me a little.

"No," my stupid mind thought in that second that he would be amused with my low endurance, especially since he's the one that put in all of the efforts.

"Good, cause I'm not nearly done with you yet."

Thirsty for you

My eyes felt heavy, but knowing that he's here pushed me to open them faster than I normally would.

His arms were wrapped around me almost uniting us as one.

I looked up without moving my head and noticed that his eyes were closed. Funny since he doesn't normally need sleep.

I decided to study his features. His masculine jawline was covered by a short stubble defining his thick lips, making it almost impossible not to claim them.

As if he read my mind, he pulled me closer, covering my mouth with his and sneaking in his tongue so it could dance with mine.

"I thought you didn't need sleep," I managed to say between kisses.

"I do rest from time to time… more like a trance state. I don't need it as often as humans do. I must admit for the last couple of years I've been entering my dream state every night, just so that I could see you. But you, waking up right now to find me staring at you would be a little weird, so I decided to close my eyes for a while."

"Is that what you're going to be doing *every night* from now on?" the thought of restraining him in this manner somehow scared me.

"I haven't thought about that yet. I guess I'll probably get some work done while you sleep, but I'd like to be here when you wake up. I really love the idea of *every night.*"

"What are you planning for us today?" I quivered at the thought that we could spend the rest of the day here, but my thoughts were quickly interrupted "Sarah, I need a drink," he growled getting out of bed and rushing to the living room.

I quickly followed him, looking at his trembling hands as he was drinking the so needed blood.

With every sip he was calming down as Damien was taking back control from the monster. But he was suffering, and it hurt me to my limit, letting a *dangerous idea* form in my mind.

"Are you ok?" I asked, approaching him to finally let my head rest on his chest.

"I haven't felt so good in centuries," he answered, letting his hand intertwine in my hair while one of his fingers gently caressed the back of my head.

"I'll have it under control soon. I can feel it. You make me weak, but also give me strength. I just need some time to acclimatize. I haven't felt these urges...this primordial thirst for blood ever since I first became a vampire."

"Is it better now?" I hesitantly asked, knowing that the blood must have calmed him down.

"I need to test it to make sure," he smiled, pulling the strap of my bra over my shoulder and letting it fall on the side.

"I need my clothes," I stopped him, realizing that if I let him continue, we'd probably end up spending the whole day locked in.

"If you didn't notice, my goal was to take the clothes off you, not put more on," he chuckled laying a hand over my waist and securing my position next to him.

Vrrrrrr... My phone vibrated, breaking the *magic* of the moment. He let out a growl of disapproval, but let me go so I could see who was calling me.

It was Lala who was interrupting us. I had a feeling from the start that it was her since she's the only person I know that could have picked such *perfect* timing.

"I want *explicit details*!" the voice on the other end spoke in her typical way.

"Hello to you too," I muttered, but in a way I was expecting this.

"Cut the small talk. Details I said...and a picture of his ass," my lunatic friend insisted.

"You do know that sharp hearing is a trait that vampires share..." Damien grinned, taking embarrassment to a new level.

"I know that you weren't home last night. I stopped by your place this morning and you weren't there." At least she can still walk in the daylight. That's a good thing.

"We'll talk about this tomorrow." I desperately tried to save the situation before Damien overhears every dirty thought that runs through Lala's mind, because they're *a lot* of them.

"Adam was saying something about the four of us having dinner together tomorrow night. He was going to run it by Damien."

"I'll give him a call a little later," Damien spoke from the corner of the room.

"Stop eavesdropping!" I muttered, knowing that from now on my *privacy* is almost history.

"I told you, super hearing... amongst other things," he smiled heading towards the kitchen.

"Lala... Not over the phone. Dinner tomorrow night with or without the guys."

"Deal. We'll talk *details* tomorrow. I need to get ready anyway, Adam is coming to pick me up for drinks in a few hours."

"Drinks?! What time is it?" I asked a little confused since I couldn't see outside.

"6 pm. You are aware that you have a watch on your phone, right?!" now she was the *smart* one.

"See you tomorrow, crazy!" I cut her short, knowing that if I'd explain that I just got up, she would probably start the interrogation a day early.

Finally, free from my personal interrogator, I made my way to the kitchen where Damien was making me coffee.

"Have you exorcised the demon yet?" I asked, looking at the expresso machine that was functioning properly this time.

"This one was worse than an actual demon," he smiled, pulling out a chair so that I could sit.

"I hope that was one of your jokes." I arranged myself at the kitchen table, unsure of whether he was kidding or not.

"Hope is a dangerous thing," he placed the coffee cup in front of me and grabbed a chair.

"So, I shouldn't have high hopes about things in general?... About this?", I looked directly into his eyes. Even if he still intimidated me, I was expecting an answer.

"About *us*? That's what you're referring to?" straight to the point.

"Yes," I gave him a short answer, knowing that there was no point in dragging out this conversation.

"I'm not a child, Sarah. Far from it. I know exactly what I want. You're moving in tonight. I think it's safe to say that we don't need hope. This is a *certitude*."

I had no words left to say, even though I could always think of a comeback line, this time I was muted. I just stood there like a dumb child, trying to realize once again that this is now my world. I'm not just reading *the book*, I'm living it.

"Do you want us to have dinner tomorrow with Adam and Lala?" I asked, trying to change the subject.

"We'll go only if you want too," he answered a little uncertainly.

"He's your friend. Don't you want us spending time with them?"

"I do. I just haven't been to that many *dinners with friends* in a while. I had a few dinners with him, but they were more like meals."

"Meals?!" my innocent side surfaced, but I quickly figured out what he was saying.

"You don't want to know," he hurriedly assured me.

"No, I don't," I finally had an idea what he was talking about. In any case, I didn't want to hear about Damien's nocturnal adventures. I've seen enough in the tabloids to know that I could be spared the details.

"Should I let him know that we're having dinner tomorrow?" he asked waiting for my confirmation.

"Yes, just emphasize on *dinner*," I muttered a little upset that Damien had touched another woman during his centuries of roaming the earth. *I never said that I'm not selfish.*

"Stop pouting and get dressed before I remove the few remaining clothes you have on," he devilishly smiled, pulling his chair a little closer.

"Club outfit or cocktail dress?" I chuckled, referring to the only two outfits I had there, then ran to the door.

"Whatever comes out faster," he called after me, making me laugh.

I went into the bedroom and put on the clothes I had at the club. I just hope I don't have any snooping neighbor who will notice that I'm coming back to my apartment two days later with the same clothes on.

"I need to feed you." Damien came from behind me and grabbed my waist, burying his head on my shoulder. It felt so personal, so good, just like he belongs there.

"Clothes first, food after," I almost whined feeling his hands moving on my body, but I really needed my clothes and makeup, plus a few files from work that I needed to study.

"We'll stop at a restaurant on the way there. I'm not negotiating this. You haven't eaten in almost 24 hours," he growled, letting me know who really is in charge.

"Fine," I rolled my eyes like the big spoiled brat I really am, let-

THIRSTY FOR YOU | 163

ting him think that I am the one doing him a favor.

"Come!" he growled, taking my hand and leading me to the front door, then to the elevator.

I pressed the button to close the doors, but his hand came over mine, turning me to face him.

"I hope you know that you raise in me more *sensations* than the thirst for blood. ***I'm also thirsty for you.***"

Senses of purity

"Behave." I seductively whispered like I was luring him to do just the opposite of that.

His tongue pushed my lips to part, but as soon as they did, so did the elevator doors, reminding us that we picked the worse possible timing.

"Mr. Arion," the security guard bowed his head as Damien and I passed him by. *My* vampire didn't respond but gave him a cold look like he was the one to blame for our interruption.

"I need to feed you," he repeated as we got into the car, like he was trying to convince himself that some urges can wait.

I can't deny that he didn't have a strong effect on me as my legs were instinctively closing so that they could diminish the drive to have him. My mouth became dry without his, dreaming of the moment we'll return to his bedroom.

"We're here," he said pulling onto the restaurant's driveway. He looked into my eyes and curved the corner of his lips as if he knew what I was thinking.

We went inside to eat dinner. He also ordered, just so he could keep me company whilst I was enjoying my dinner.

It's the small gestures of a grand man that makes my heart skip a beat.

Even though initially we were in a *hurry*, things calmed down during the time spent there. We started talking about our likes and dislikes, from the way I like my coffee to the way food tasted five centuries ago.

The thought of leaving my home was settling in as I move towards a new part of my life.

We finished dinner and finally drove towards my apartment.

He parked in front of the building and took a bottle out of his car's trunk before we went up.

"Are you ok?" I asked the moment we reached my apartment.

"Yes, I just need a glass," he gently spoke, making me realize that dinner must have been hell for him.

I rushed to give him one, and after a few sips a smile appeared on his face.

"I'm still not completely used to the effect you have on me," he spoke, stroking my cheek with the back of his index finger.

"Just relax while I get some of my things together. I would offer you water or coffee, but I know that you don't need it."

"I must be a keeper, low maintenance," he chuckled, letting out a softer version of him.

I headed towards the bedroom while he stayed behind carefully studying every corner of my apartment. I was a little embarrassed since things weren't left in a great state the last time I was here as cleaning was the last thing on my mind.

"I didn't get to clean."... *I was too busy mopping around after you*- I left the final part out.

"This seems so familiar" he spoke entering the room then leaned on the wall next to the door.

I took an empty suitcase out of the dressing room, threw it on the bed and started to fill it with a selection of my clothes while Damien was carefully studying every last corner of my room.

I was a little busy trying to figure out what to take with me when I felt him behind me. His fingers were wandering through my stacks of clothes as if he was trying to learn everything there is to know about me.

Suddenly, he stopped because something else caught his attention. A shopping bag that left unopened from a very famous woman's lingerie store.

"Was this for me?" he asked lifting with one finger a very sexy teddy from the bag.

I didn't answer but turned to face him only to catch his lustful eyes meandering my body.

"Put it on!" he ordered then left the small room to go into the bedroom.

If it would have been any other person I would have reposted. No one should have the audacity to tell me what to do, but with him it's something else. His command doesn't enrage me, on the contrary, it raises some kind of fervor to please him.

I took off my clothes, then slipped into the lace lingerie, arranging myself in the mirror for more than a few minutes.

I was so nervous because even though the relaxed version of Damien sets me into a sort of normality, the intense version of him reminds me that we're *nowhere near that.*

He is neither man nor demon, but a flawless combination between decent and immoral, letting lust and sin intertwine between *faded senses of purity.*

I stepped into the room and his eyes started glinting with excitement.

I noticed how his glass and the bottle were sitting peacefully on my nightstand. He probably got them while I was changing to help him appease his *thirst.*

I stood in front of the dressing room door while he took a seat on the bed, running his hands over the silk sheets.

"Did you feel me here, on this bed?" he asked in a husky voice, instantly forming a knot in my stomach and a throb between my thighs.

I didn't reply, but my feet carried me to the bed where they instinctively wrapped around him, leaving no space between his growing arousal and my flesh.

He grabbed my waist, then quickly moved towards my breasts where he stopped for a second, taking a deep breath.

I gasped as he continued his way up until he reached the back of my head and wrapped one of his arms around a strand of my hair. He pulled it passionately, forcing me to face him. "Did you feel me, Sarah?" he asked again, making my bottom lip shiver before I could answer.

He pulled me gently so that I fell back a little, resting on his arm. His other hand followed the lace's path, moving between my waist and my chest.

He was taking control of my body as every single part of me started pulsing with the rush of him.

"Don't fight it," he whispered. My arms were becoming limp and I was losing control of any remaining voluntary movement, but my senses were intensifying to a whole new level. Our lips became as one as his tongue was studying every last corner of my mouth.

He was slowly changing everything that I ever thought I wanted in life.

I could feel how my teddy was sliding off my body as the cool silk that had been caressing my skin was being replaced by his soft gentle kisses.

Hearing me moan softly, he stopped and decided to turn his attention to other parts of my body.

He lifted me up so that he could change my position on the bed allowing him to be on top.

Having absolutely no control was worrying me a little, so an almost undetectable growl escaped my mouth, making Damien pick up on my discomfort.

"Shush," his hand promptly descended from my hips to the place in between them, imprisoning my flesh, then spoiling it with circled movements.... *like someone could "shush" while he was doing that.*

"Ahhh"-a moan found its way to his ears, a vicious smile spread over his face.

"What did I say?!" he growled while biting one of my lips then descended to attend *other* parts of my body.

"Free me!" I whined, unable to move and more convinced than ever that I may not resist what was coming my way.

He smirked and placed a hand on my lower abdomen, sending a jolt of energy that combined with his other actions making my entire body shudder with an intensity I could barely withstand.

At this point, even if he'd lost the grip he had on me, it wouldn't be of much use since with just a few tricks he had left my body almost motionless. I really need to practice my endurance and I sensed that no time will be spared on doing so.

"This damn bed," he growled, slipping inside and releasing his grip on my arms only so I could wrap them around his neck.

He started moving slow but hard, owning every inch of me and exploring new limits.

His mouth hungrily searched for mine as the place where we *first met* was coming to life. The room was practically starting to move from his gestures.

"The neighbors," I realized as the sounds of the bed *walking* through the room could be overheard in at least other five apartments in the building. *Shit, I think even my 80-year-old neighbor knows his name by now.*

"I'll buy the building," he answered. Unsure if he was joking or not, we continued in a much more alert rhythm, reminding me of who he is. This man isn't used to obeying others' will, but his will was to be obeyed by others and keeping things down was definitely not on the books for us tonight.

He continued at this unearthly level until my body literally caved in. I could barely keep my eyes open, resting my head on his chest and surrendering to all beautiful dreams he's creating.

"Vesnic a mea"- (forever mine)," he whispered letting his words resonate in my mind removing any shadow of doubt that his heart now belonged to me.

Walls of my heart

I could feel him leaving the bed as I forced my eyes to open and follow his shadowy image around the room.

I remained silent, watching him approach the window and rest his hands on the window still.

He just stood there in silence, glancing at the sun that was slowly rising, lifting its rays over the building. The more I looked at him, the more his stillness started to hurt. The pounding at the *walls of my heart* was transferring his pain and making it my own to the point that I felt like the bed was trying to burst into flames under me.

He finally started pulling the blinds down, bringing *darkness* back to the room... letting **his darkness** *flood the room.*

"Do you miss the light?" I asked, foolishly believing that there could possibly be a different answer than what my heart was telling me.

"I used to imagine letting the rays in just to be able to see the beauty of a sunrise for one last time. This is not a blessing, but a curse. Having to walk forever in darkness, knowing that I could hurt the one I love... the thirst, the emptiness...the desperation created. It sometimes consumes me," he spoke while the last flicker dawns light was fading in his eyes.

Something started tormenting me. A mystical force born from the desperate need to heal him. To extinguish his misery and drown it in the depths of the eternity that was hunting him.

I jumped out of the bed as a dark power came over me. There was a need to close the wounds on his soul "I'm here now," I whispered, claiming his lips.

Damien

I've never been like this before... shown any kind of weakness in front of another person, yet I've done it with her. I've let her know my true human side and I don't feel exposed, just safe. She's the only one in the world that would never feed on my suffering. I feel like she's desperately trying to extinguish it.

She was slowly pushing me towards her bed and I was more than a little impressed by her spectacular recovery after last night. I found it more than intriguing since no other woman in centuries had tried such a gesture after only sleeping for two hours.

I fought the urge to take control, curious to see what she had in mind and secretly grateful for the bottle I just finished before she woke up.

She was purring between kisses, but as I was preparing to lay down and enjoy whatever she had in mind, I caught a glimpse of the silk sheets from the corner of my eyes.

A dark stain forming the contour of her body was covering the white sheets.

It was ash. Small burns on the surface of the bed as if she'd almost burst into flames, probably from drawing my pain onto herself. But no normal Amplifier could do this before she'd chose sides.

Has she done it already? Decided to become a witch? Because no vampire had bitten her and there couldn't be any other logical explanation for the ash.

I shook my head, trying to chase these thoughts away. There had to be another rational explanation, but I may be a little too distracted to come up with one.

For a moment I feared that she would notice the marks, but the light was too dim for her to be able to see this, while my eyes were already accustomed to a life of darkness.

I took my mind off it for now, turning my full attention to the way she was trying to *heal* me. It was amusing and bitter at the same time since I know deep down, she will never be able to do so. She will *never* be able to chase away the true darkness inside of me and I will **never** *allow her* to join me in it.

Her lips were moving so rapidly on mine as I laid on the bed and my waist became a prisoner of her thighs.

She pressed me into the mattress, letting the little white robe that lightly covered her slip down and expose her completely naked body.

My first instinct was to take control. I wouldn't normally enjoy this experience since the dominance instinct is a defining feature of my inner beast. But her fervor made me stop to enjoy this shift of powers.

As she pulled my boxers down the sound of my scratching teeth betrayed me and made her slow her movements.

I took a nervous break, unsure if I should reach for the glass or not. I noticed her smile as she was becoming mine, the gray clouds evaporated and the intense sensation of our bodies uniting evaporated any dangerous thought.

She moved so naturally, as if she knew every inch of me and every action needed to mesmerize me.

Unable to resist her long sways, I captured her hips trying to stall any rushed reaction on my end.

She fought it at first, still trying to keep her rhythm, but my grip was much stronger than her will.

I gave myself a little time to win back my body that was one step away from betraying me.

With a swift motion, I grabbed her neck and brought her lips to join mine while my other hand rested on the small of her back, keeping it in a fixed position while I started moving from underneath her. She let out a little growl of discomfort since things weren't going her way, but soon her eyes widened, meeting my vicious smile.

She tried to move but didn't stand a chance. My thrusts grew in intensity until I could feel her entire body trembling, smothered by my kisses.

Barely breathing she tried to free herself, even for a second, pushing her knees into the bed until I almost lost my grip on her. She must have caught me in a moment of weakness because her strength could never compare even with the force I hold in one finger.

Even though questions were starting to form in the corners of my mind, I chased them away again and focused on the moment.

As she probably thought she found victory I grabbed her and turn her back onto the bed while I regained my rightful place in her core.

She smiled, then pouted sensing the immediate *trouble.*

Sarah

This man can't be controlled. I learned that this morning as every one of my attempts was smothered.

His pleasure was of a devilish nature, making me enjoy but also fear his immortal stamina.

I think it was well past noon before I woke up, this time in his arms without being forced to search for him in the corners of the room like this morning.

I snuggled up on his chest for a few more minutes until my body and my physical needs took their toll. I was forced to use the bathroom and dispose of the few liquids that remained in my bladder.

As I returned to the room and turned on the light a cold chill sneaked in me when I saw the burn marks on the sheet. I hoped that Damien had caused that as a reaction from the peak of our time of passion, but something inside me told me that wasn't true.

"Damien?!" the uncertainty in my trembling voice made him jump out of bed and bring me the warmth and comfort of his body.

"I did that, didn't I?" I could barely speak, unsure of my powers, and most of all unsure of what I am anymore.

"I had no idea you were this strong. I've felt a small part of it on previous days, but never imagined that it could be at this intensity."

"What's wrong with me?" I asked, a little scared that he may know the answer.

"Nothing is wrong. I just think that you're different. Your emotions or intense feelings come alive and enhance your normal strength. Has this ever happened before?"

"No, only when I'm around you... I... I never felt like this before," I murmured, admitting that he has a special power over me. In a way, I think he already knew that.

"Don't worry, you'll be able to control it in time. It's probably because you're an Amplifier and your half is a vampire," he spoke with a casual tone that I didn't *fully buy.*

"Just let me know if things get too heated while I'm next to you. We wouldn't want to burn the house down," he joked, trying to reduce the danger of the situation.

"I think it's time for you to pack. We're meeting Adam and Lala for dinner, remember?" he asked, stroking my arm with the back of his index finger.

"Right away, but I need a coffee and to grab a bite first." All that effort had given me quite an appetite and there were more than a few hours until dinner.

Heading towards the kitchen I suddenly remembered that there was nothing in the fridge. Anything that was lurking inside would have probably be out of date by now anyway. It was going to be either crackers, starvation...or pizza. That's actually a good idea.

"Let's call for pizza," I told him. I was already dreaming for the moment my doorbell would ring and a hot steamy slice would find its way to my belly.

"Believe it or not, I never called for pizza." Damien giggled, making me laugh.

"Prosciutto Crudo and Fungi, the number is on the fridge. There's a first time for everything. I'm going to make coffee" I said walking past him and collecting a mug from the counter.

It was so funny to watch Damien as my normality had such a different meaning to him. It made me wonder if I'd enjoy the times when I'll no longer needed coffee, food, or other mortal's necessities. The was no doubt about it, *the day I'll join him in eternity is coming fast.*

I packed a few things while I was waiting, then enjoyed my slices of Italian heaven. He joined me, probably wondering how he didn't find out about this pizza place earlier. I know that he doesn't need to eat, but it doesn't mean he can't enjoy a nice tasty meal.

I kept looking at him and wondered how food used to taste back in the days, how he lived and about every single joy or sorrow, he went through without me by his side. But most important... *How will our life be from now on?*

Dinner from hell

I had finally packed everything I needed. Even though Damien insisted that I only take what's absolutely necessary and we will buy the rest, my *necessary* barely fit in his car.

The sight of him carrying my bags to the car amused me. I had imagined him having servants around him doing the useless *human* activities, while his royal self could only be occupied with matters of great importance.

For a few moments I thought I may have been wrong. But when we reached his apartment building the guards almost fell over each other's feet to empty the car and deliver all bags to the apartment.

He smirked, knowing that his air of supremacy raised deep emotions inside me. Even though I hate to admit it, what I love about him most of all is that he isn't common. You can tell he is apart even if he's surrounded by a thousand other men. An aura of mystery enfolds him. Even though I've unlocked the biggest one, I still feel that I'm far from done discovering his secrets.

"Are you daydreaming?" he asked sneaking behind me and letting one of his hands slips against my thigh.

I jumped a little, being snapped out of my reverie quickly finding my place in his arms.

"Dinner" I shook my head as I was slipping back into one of his spells.

"Dinner...." he muttered and left for the bedroom to get changed.

I followed, amused by his grumpy mood. He's always used to getting his way... that's until he met me.

I was ready in around 20 minutes, but as I finished my makeup and left the bathroom, I almost stopped breathing.

Damien was concentrating on closing his shirt sleeves buttons while my eyes examined him from his elegant shoes to his custom made black dress pants and onto the shirt that wrapped his torso, letting the defined shapes of his muscles sneak from underneath it.

I approached him and arranged a loose strand of his hair that decided to rebel while he was adjusting his shirt. Taken by surprise his breathing quickened and his eyes started glittering shades of red. He pushed me aside and went straight to the living room to suppress his thirst.

I found him cursing, probably because he couldn't still his inhuman drives yet.

"Damien?!" I called out to him a little worried but keeping my distance this time.

"It's ok now," he answered as his breathing was getting steadier.

"You're just too beautiful," he smiled gently, approaching me and stretching out his hand. "Shall we?"

I reached for his palm and let him guide me to the door then drove off to Adam's place.

"Stop worrying, I'm fine now," he muttered, keeping his eyes on the road. I didn't say a word, but I guess he could tell from the way I was tossing and turning on the seat.

"You looked so beautiful when you came into the room that you took me by surprise, I didn't have time to prepare myself."

"I'll wear a bag over my head, next time"- I giggled and at the same time made him understand that I'm getting more accustomed to this life with each passing day.

He parked in the Count's alley and opened the car door for me. "No bag can keep these away from me," he muttered, approaching me then slowly grazing my lips with his teeth. Taking me by my hand he showed me to a small door a few feet away from the club entrance.

The small old wooden door that greeted us reminded me of the times it came from and strengthening my feeling of home. *A world where I belonged.*

We took the stairs up until we reached a big lobby that resembled the bars' architecture. Brick and wood decorated the walls while dimmed lighting revealed a few old paintings that fascinated me. They all depicted different wars over various periods in time, but all had one thing in common, *vampires.* Every canvas illustrated a battle in which the humans looked terrified, crushed by hundreds of vampires in their search for blood.

There was another element that drew my full attention, their commander. A tall dark-haired vampire with ruby eyes that seemed to burn through his victims. All the drawings depicted him as a leader, an evil demon that suppressed mankind. I knew him in a different image, for me he wasn't a monster, he was just Damien.

"Something's wrong." he growled shifting his nose as if he just caught an unfamiliar scent... *Or maybe the problem was it was too familiar.*

"Lala!" I got scared and headed straight to the door located at the end of the lobby.

"No, we're leaving!" Damien grabbed at my arm but my hand escaped his grip. I started to pound at the entrance while he looked at me a little confused.

A few moments later Lala slowly opened the door, remaining in its shadow like she was giving me time to accustom.

Stepping inside, I was struck by how pale her face was compared to her normal rosy complexion. I immediately started staring at the turtle neck dress that she had chosen for the night.

I felt so sickened and frightened inside. For some time I was in a state of denial. I kept hoping that this wasn't true, that my mind was playing tricks on me and all the signs were only in my imagination.

I couldn't move. Even though Damien was in the lobby he was unable to enter the apartment because of me. There was an awkward moment of silence, so unusual for Laura since she was always so cheerful and knew how to make her presence felt the second you stepped into a room with her.

This time it was very different. She just kept looking at me like she was trying to get accustomed to me. I felt Damien's palms wrapping around my arms like he was getting ready to pull me aside.

"Relax! Breathe slowly," Adam's voice came from across the room and I notice him heading towards Lala.

What has he done?

That was the question that was desperately scratching the walls of my mind. I didn't take long to confirm what I already knew from the second I stepped into the loft. Something started pounding inside of me. A power fueled with hate that began controlling all of my senses and for a second turned me into someone else.

Adam didn't get to reach Lala because in a second, I sprang across the room and both hands wrapped around Adam's neck, pinning him to the floor.

I imagined myself draining all the life out of him and eagerly waited until I could hear his neck-breaking so I could snap his head right off his shoulders.

I was in another world where the desperate screams of Lala and the commanding voice of Damien couldn't reach me. It was just me and my target. The man who had to pay with his life for claiming my friend's.

I was so close to reaching my goal when Damien wrapped his arms around me, trying to pull me away. I shifted my body, trying to break free and involuntarily threw him three feet away, breaking one of the table chairs with his fall.

I stopped, scared of what I had just done and devastated that I could hurt him.

He got up looking at me. As soon as he realized that, I snapped out of my *delirium*. He caught me in an embrace, holding me still as I crashed in his arms.

"It's ok, I've got you," he kept whispering while kissing me and stroking my hair at the same time. I remained there for a few minutes until I was able to stand on my own.

"What have you done?!" Damien growled so loud that the walls vibrated with his words.

Adam didn't answer, probably still in shock because a mortal had almost killed him with her bare hands.

"I agreed!" Lala rushed to assure us while getting in front of him in a useless attempt to defend him.

"Why would you do something like that? You know him for less than a week." I couldn't help but express my repulsion towards this whole situation, especially since I suspected him of working his unnatural charms to get her to agree.

"I told you not to touch her! *You agreed that you won't touch her!*" Damien roared again making Adam's face to become even paler.

"I have... I have feelings for her," Adam mumbled from across the room. Anyone who really knew him could confirm this was a man that feared nothing, but somehow the fact that he disobeyed Damien terrified him.

"You have feelings for her?! You haven't had feelings for anyone for a half a century, but you decided to develop *feelings* for Sarah's best friend?!" Damien's fangs were showing while I couldn't decide if I should stop him or help him kill Adam.

"I don't know how it happened; you know me. I wouldn't have done something like this unless I was sure. I turned her so we could be together." Adam tried to explain while Damien was approaching him.

"Please!" Lala screamed, holding her stomach and almost collapsing.

Adam didn't waste a second practically running through Damien to catch her, then just like he was unphased by us, took a blood glass from the counter and pressed it on Lala's lips making sure she slowly ingested it.

Damien remained still, but as I watched carefully what happened I realized it was true. Even though Adam was afraid of the consequences he didn't hesitate for a second to take care of Laura. The worried look imprinted on his face, waiting for her to recover, reminded me of me. I shared that look when I discovered the discomfort I had provoked in Damien. A worry that can only come from the depths of pure feelings.

Adam stayed with her for a few moments until she regained her powers, then he turned to face us.

"I didn't know this would happen when I asked you here to dinner yesterday. It was done in an impulse. You know me." Lala explained. She kept her distance from me since I presume my hot blood caused her dizziness.

"You should've known better!" Damien muttered looking at Adam.

"Don't get me wrong. It was an impulse, but I don't regret it." Lala explained.

"We wanted to tell you over diner, but I didn't think Sarah would figure it out even before she'd enter the room." Adam intervened.

"I admit, I got a little carried away. I should have waited a while, but this doesn't change anything. We chose to be together and this would have happened sooner or later. So, don't judge me for something you're going to do yourself," Adam muttered.

"Apparently you don't know me well enough." Damien turned his back on him and returned to me checking again to see if I'm ok. His hand rested on my face while his eyes searched mine for answers I didn't have.

I took a deep breath and tried to accustom myself with the idea that what was done was done. But as that thought rested in my mind, the memory that I threw a vampire across the room became vivid. I can't comprehend how this happened and from Damien's look neither does he.

"I think we all need a drink before dinner." Lala giggled in her characteristic way, trying to ease the atmosphere. At least she didn't lose herself with this transformation. As I get more accustomed to the idea, I'm starting to think the *mistress of darkness* part suits her perfectly.

"I'm sorry, it's not my place to judge your lives, but you have to understand that she's my friend and the news came as a shock. Everything is happening so fast that is overwhelming me." I tried to explain myself to Adam even though I couldn't justify my behavior.

Seeing me more relaxed, I felt Damien loosen up and after drinking the glass Lala offered, he almost returned to his normal state.

The dinner turned into just a few more drinks. I didn't want to force everyone to eat just to please me, besides, I had lost my appetite the moment I came through the door anyway.

Damien was still a little uneasy about everything. I couldn't decide if it had to do with the fact that Adam indirectly had made me suffer or with the fact that he defied him. He may have given up the privilege of leadership, but his royal attitude burst through his every pore.

I realized that this was one of those crucial moments when you can build or break a friendship. I wasn't going to let Lala go just because she prefers liquid food these days.

Once she got more comfortable with my presence she unwound and her jokes brought smiles back to our faces, especially since she started telling us all how this had happened because of a little *bedroom fun.* We had to cover our ears to be spared all of the details.

Things were almost normal for a few hours until Adam decided to ask the question that lingered on everyone's lips, but no one dared to set free: *"What are you, Sarah?"*

 The King

What am I?

How can I answer that when I have no idea myself?

"I'm sorry, I guess I wasn't expecting an actual answer from you since I believe you're confused yourself," Adam explained, but without easing my mind.

"I hoped you know since you've carefully studied our history" Damien was showing concern about my situation for the second time.

"Did this ever happen before?" Adam inquired, trying to make sense of everything.

"I almost burned the sheets this morning," I stuttered.

"I always knew you were hot!" Lala said, making us all laugh and eased the atmosphere.

"See why I had to keep her? She's more alive than all us vampires put together." Adam looked at her like he'd been waiting his whole life to find her.

"Well, now that you *found her,* you better take good care of her because I promise that if something happens to my friend because of what you did, I **AM** going to kill you," I muttered and something deep inside of me was telling me that this wasn't an unfounded threat.

"I wouldn't want you to unleash your powers on me, so I promise to take good care of Laura," Adam joked, but was at the same time also a little worried. I could feel it from the tone of his voice and from the way he was shifting looks with Damien who pulled my chair closer to him so he could rest his hand on my thigh.

"I already explained to her that she's an Amplifier, but I'm afraid that's as far as I can go because I've never before met someone who developed powers without choosing sides."

"These things... our *gifts* come from unexplained sources, and as in your case, your abilities are greater than other vampires'. Maybe that happened with her too and she will reach full power after she makes a decision." Adam's explanation brought me only concern and the not relief I was hoping for.

"I wasn't born with special aptitudes. I developed them over time with training and self-composure," Damien muttered.

"Damien, I saw you single-handedly destroy an entire army. Training or not, no other vampire did that before. Obviously, the dosage of power isn't the same for everyone and you both drew the longer stick. We can only wait and find out how long it is in Sarah's case. One thing that I am absolutely sure about is that no other vampires mustn't get to her.

If she does indeed have greater powers than any known Amplifier before and if one of our own drinks her blood, it could lead to catastrophic consequences.

I'm sorry to say this, but she could be a *weapon* in the wrong hands."

Damien didn't say a word but reflected on everything Adam explained, then in a gesture of pure madness took my hand and almost dragged me across the room, through the lobby, down the stairs and then into the club.

All vampire's eyes were on us from the moment we stepped inside, but that's exactly what he wanted.

We made our way through them, quickly followed by Adam and Lala who couldn't hide their confused looks.

....and then it happened. The king was taking back his throne, in the strongest possible way to attempt to protect what's his... ME.

"Look at her!"- he growled and all vampire's gazes turned, studying me the way I used to examine priceless relics.

"A few of you may not know who I am, but I assure you that you don't want to know me better than tonight because you won't live to tell the story of our encounter.

For those that do know me, you realize that now is a crucial moment to pay attention.

I'm not going to repeat myself. If you have any doubt of what can happen if you disobey me, you can step forward and I can gladly remove it right now... *Along with your head.*

She is **my** property, therefore anyone who even dreams of touching her, anyone who even gets near her, will die!

The same rule applies to anyone that doesn't defend her when needed to. I know that there'll be a few who will probably take this just as an idle threat. I trust the others who know what I'm capable of will put them in their place or else I'm coming after all of you.

On no account think that the last 500 years have numbed my senses, on the contrary, they sharpened them.

If you *feared* me back then you should be *mortified* now!

Does anyone in this room not recognize me as their leader?" Damien growled, bringing terror in all of the eyes looking at him.

One by one they bowed in front of him and to my surprise, Adam and Lala didn't fail to follow the rest. Everyone recognized him as their leader, except for one.

In the corner of the room there was a person who dared to defy him, Joseph.

Damien measured him with despise and I knew he was ready for a direct battle.

He disrespected Damien and that could only mean Joseph represented a danger to me and he couldn't have that.

Damien's fists clenched. Before he could react, obeying their King's command all vampire's eyes turned on Joseph, preparing for an attack.

Outnumbered and backed into a corner, he took a deep breath and slowly started to descend until his knees touched the ground and his head bowed, recognizing Damien's authority.

"Share the word to others not present here tonight and **kill** anyone who dares to oppose!" Damien growled, then took my hand like before and showed me to the car.

***

"Do you think they'll listen in the long run?" I asked him as I opened the cabinet in the living room to pour him a glass.

This gesture wasn't bothering me, on the contrary, it soothed me knowing that it will help calm him down.

"You don't know me how some of them do. When I ruled before I used to be merciless, you may even say inhumane.

I promised myself that I won't ever go back there, but I would do it for you.

I was absolutely and completely serious with them all. If anyone would dare touch you, I would wipe them from the face of the earth."

"Why didn't you do this on the night you found me at The Count?"

"I didn't want to claim this role. To be honest, I didn't see the real threat. I kept thinking about how this may impact you... *us*. But tonight, when I realized your true powers and what they could do, I knew that I had to step up and publicly claim you and my place amongst them.

I know all about what this kind of power can accomplish in the wrong hands. I used to own the powers *and the wrong kind of hands*.

I was one step away from wiping the human race off the face of the earth."

"But you stopped, that says something about you too."

"Only with a great sacrifice," he spoke with a sadness that even pressed down upon my own heart.

"Drink!" I asked him, eager to see him relax and put this evening behind us.

"You didn't ask me if you're safe to leave," he whispered, emptying the glass.

"That's because I don't want to be in any other place but here." I took a breath, then crushing my lips on his and feeling the taste of blood in his mouth.

For a second it made me so aware of what he really is. A king, a beast, a killer.... *the man I love.*

I didn't hesitate and let my tongue dance with his, more intoxicated by this power than ever before.

He caught my jaw with one of his hands and kissed me with such intensity that it sent shivers all around my body. He was in total control tonight. He could break all the rules and the monster inside wouldn't dare defy him because, in the end, his greater power came from *Damien the man.*

He let out a long growl and pushed me towards the couch, whilst managing to remove every single piece of clothing that covered me before I could feel the leather material beneath me.

He wasted no time removing his garments either and with a swift move claimed me as his again, letting our bodies intertwine in countless hours of passion until my human nature caved in front of his immortal resistance.

I lived for every moment with him. The pleasure his body brings and the pain his hands sometimes unwillingly provoke while traveling my flesh. Only together are we *complete.*

Things were finally neither good nor bad, but somehow we found a balance. A middle ground where not all questions needed answers and the moment mattered more than the eternity. But fate spares no one and doesn't care about tormented souls. The only thing that matters is that the cards align in the grand game that was prepared for us. Little did we know that at this time *the cards* **weren't** *in our favor.*

Pure bliss

We stayed in NY for a few more months.

With Damien's help tracing valuable art pieces, Karla was almost building me statues of recognition. But deep down I despised her for the way she acted when I first met Damien. Her thirst for his money gave life to a repulsion inside of me, which in time only grew larger with each one of her greedy gestures.

It was time to move on. If before I couldn't dream of such accomplishment, with Damien's help I opened an art dealership business in Manhattan. I called it "The Breathe Galleries" since it was a part of the past breathed into the present.

It was a huge success with its luxurious parties in which some of the elderly vampires increased their fortunes and the elite of NY expanded their art collection.

In only a few short weeks I became respected in both worlds. Everyone knew my name and a few paparazzi photos of me and Damien got me to the front covers of all the important tabloids.

We didn't like that intrusion, especially since the unwanted attention could get Damien into trouble. It was only a matter of time until people would start raising questions about his appearances only being nocturnal and even though some celebrities prefer the nightlife, they still get caught sunbathing on some remote island or traveling the oceans in some overpriced yacht.

It was a risk I wasn't willing to take just for my moment of glory and I never enjoyed the spotlight anyway. I wanted to be someone to the people that mattered, not for some superficial person who would probably analyze my every face feature before reading about my real achievements. Even though NY was home for both of us we decided to take a small break from the agitation a metropolis provided.

With all my employees instructed, because, yes, I was the *boss* now, we packed and decided to live in Europe for a while. Leaving Adam and Lala was a little difficult since we used to share most evenings with them when in NY. However, with their flexible schedule we made more than a few visiting arrangements

Our first stop was in Italy. As Sicily was a little too sunny for his preferences, we decided on Venice. A city that seemed to be somehow undisturbed by the passing of time. The dark narrow alleys held the same beauty as the sun rising from the ocean.

Even though I still went out during the day to resolve earthly necessities, like visits to the bank or who knows what fiscal agency, the light started to have less importance to me.

I loved floating around in gondolas while Damien shared stories from centuries ago. Royal secrets long forgotten over time and about the true forces that stood behind every crowned head and secret organizations that really rule the world for ages.

He was as magic as every word he spoke. We ended up living in this beautiful spell. In this place he and I were the only protagonists, while all the rest were mere extras on the set of our lives.

Word had spread through the vampires and everyone bowed their head in his presence. It was funny in a way, because on several occasions when we entered different locations where humans and vampires both were present, the humans repeated the vampire's gesture. They were led by herd behavior, but without an actual idea of why they were doing it. I used to make fun of him because of that. I joked that if he'd ever decided to be humanities supreme leader, it would suffice to gather only a few important human and vampire politicians in a room and just show up. Because, yes, as he let me in secret by secret, I found out that vampires were involved in all structures and institutions around the world.

Hidden doors were opening for us, letting me into places no human has ever set foot in as Damien was facilitating my access to exclusive vampire clubs.

I listened to ancient battle songs and to sonnets by interpreters who had centuries of musical training.

His world wasn't dusky, but shined with the knowledge accumulated over eras. The darkness it provided entered through every single one of my cells making me bloom with life.

I was absorbing every little piece of his civilization and a belief that I was already one of them was burning inside. There was only one step to take so that I could *finally find my way home.*

***

We returned to NY on several occasions to check on my gallery and other businesses Damien had there. We never remained for more than a couple of weeks since discovering relics in some forgotten corner of the world was much more interesting than the respect we received in the big city.

We traveled for a while throughout Asia, the old Ethiopian territory where the vampire legends were very much alive through the villagers, then finally returned to Europe. The Victorian timeline preserved in some parts here was the period we enjoyed the most. Losing ourselves in some Croatian or Romanian castle was the perfect background for our fairytale.

In time, I found out that Damien had a lot more properties than I initially thought. After two years of visiting most of them we decided to remain for a while at an old chateau he owned in France.

It was built in a gothic style with black brick walls and long corridors. It had more rooms than we could count and although I wasn't too fond of the idea, we had to bring Margaret along as supervising the cleaning and maintenance of it would take more time than we would have.

The idea of her having a secret crush on him was somehow unable to leave my head. Even though I knew it could be only a hallucination of her mind, I wasn't pleased that she kept looking at me like I don't belong there.

Fortunately, the vineyard and the property combined were so large that there could be days or even weeks without having contact with her, especially since I started to sleep during the daytime and Damien *occupied* all my nights.

His need for blood just so he could be in my presence diminished over time and his self-control became much stronger with each new day.

At night we explored dark lanes in the cities around us, or entertained ourselves with some Shakespearian play that always ended with a theatrical bloodbath. Apparently, he was a vampire too and the *tragedies* were very appreciated by his kind since when you live for more than a few normal lifetimes you gather your own share of tragedies.

When we wanted to be truly alone, we would go in the vineyard, lay on the grass and watch the stars. The moon was our sun and we would lose ourselves for hours between the galaxies, trying to figure out where we came from. Were we a blessing or a curse? *Anomalies* or *The balance*?

Everything was perfect and in all this time there was only a single encounter that broke my equilibrium for a short period.

We were visiting a count. A very *old* acquaintance of Damien's who had developed an interest in the Aztec culture. He was willing to trade with us some of his artifacts for an ancient statue of Oxomo, the goddess of astrology. I guess that the fact the world didn't end in 2012 as they predicted didn't alter his obsession with them.

He also had a woman that took care of the property maintenance, a lot like Margaret from that point of view, but very different from all the rest.

I didn't have much contact with her, except right before we

were leaving. I accidentally dropped my bag and she rushed to help me pick it up. Our hands brushed for a split second and the familiarity and warmth of her touch made me search her face so I could have a better peek. She reminded me of Mrs. Ullmann. A smile appeared on my face while I was looking at her but I didn't find the same warmth reflected in her. Instead, I noticed a concerned look, I could say she was almost terrified of me.

After a few moments in which she couldn't wipe her shocked expression, she grabbed Damien's hand, got on her knees, and pleaded "You can't. You can't... *It* must never happen!"

Damien pulled his hand back, threw her a cold look and without asking what this was about, simply grabbed my waist and growled "We're leaving. Now!"

We never talked about this moment again. I brought it up several times but it remained the only subject he avoided. Even though I demanded to see that woman again so she could clarify things, he insisted that she was just babbling and probably had me confused with someone else.

I still thought he was keeping something from me, but with time I let it go and stopped insisting since it was clearly bothering him.

We remained there in our sanctuary. Days of pure bliss turned from months and months into years.

We lived our beautiful dream, far away from intrusive eyes, playing into the depths of the night and living with more passion than any human being. He was my king and I was his ***unproclaimed*** queen.

Eternity

"Mr. Bechard is inviting us to his Gala," I announced to Damien. As I kept re-reading the golden letters, I was reminded of a similar letter that had first brought us together.

He didn't respond at first. He was a little preoccupied because he was shaving at that time. He's always like this for a few minutes every day. I guess it has something to do with the fact that he needs to do this daily because of the much faster regenerating rhythm vampires have. Repeating the same action every evening for all eternity might get to you.

"Damien..." I got his attention by moving a finger along his back while gluing my lips on his shoulder.

"Do you want us to go?" he asked in a soft tone.

"I hate to agree with Karla, but it's a great opportunity. You know I was telling you about going to New York next week to check on things anyway."

"Ok, I had promised Adam that we would drop by soon."

"Great! I'll arrange for a private jet." We can't really fly with a normal plane and risk a delay, but when you hire a private jet no one asks about your eccentricities or why the blinds have to stay shut during the flight.

"Hurry up, there's a bottle waiting for me and after that, I will be *waiting for you,*" he growled, sending me the most seductive look he owned and making me rush to the computer to make the reservations.

My fingers glided over the keyboard, eager to be done with the outside world for tonight so that I could return to *my vampire*.

A week later- NY

"Are you ready?" I asked, rearranging my cleavage and looking for a purse in the dressing room.

"Yes," he whispered moving his hands on my thighs and exploring my neck with his lips.

He has a habit or wrinkling my dresses before we leave the house, but tonight this isn't going to happen. I prepared too much for this Gala and I didn't have time to search for another outfit.

"Not tonight," I muttered and heard him puff like a child that just lost one of his toys.

"But... when we get home-" I approached him and took his bottom lip prisoner between my own, then gave him a little peck and headed towards the door. He followed both annoyed and eager at the same time.

We got into his car and as he drove there, I relived the steps that first took me to meet him. The glamorous city lights that guided me there, the emotion formed that night and excitement that followed me in all these years spent by his side.

This time the paparazzi were interested in us, but Damien sneaked me between some celebrities. We made our way in before they could make an entire photo album of us.

As usual, everyone who was anyone was there. It wasn't long before I was mingling through the crowd and talking to different people of my interest.

I didn't drag Damien along since socializing was his least favorite activity. He stayed in Mr. Bechard's company who I recently found out was one of his own kind.

A few hours flew by and I must admit that I was starting to get tired of talking to so many people. I tried to reach the balcony but had to stop several times after being approached by different acquaintances on the way there. I even received the promise of a very important contract without even asking. All of this would have been impossible three years ago.

A little exhausted, I finally reached the balcony and to my surprise, Damien was there too.

He was talking to a woman, but I couldn't recognize her because she had her back on me.

This wouldn't normally disturb me but he had a smile on his face and hearing her giggle as I was approaching made a knot form in the pit of my stomach.

He saw me and a warmth spread across his face that would normally soothe me in seconds, but this time *it didn't*.

"Sarah, this is Damira, Mr. Bechard's daughter," he said as he pulled me next to him and wrapped one of his arms around my waist.

I looked at the woman and noticed a hint of jealousy in her eyes. Even though Damien never showed interest in any woman, it doesn't mean that women didn't show an interest in him. I wouldn't normally be bothered, but there was something about her that made me feel uncomfortable.

Soon I put two and two together and realized what it was. The fact that she was a beautiful young woman in her early twenties wasn't the thing that bothered me, neither her flawless complexion nor her perfect platinum curls that reminded me of one of those porcelain dolls. It was the fact that she had a gift I'm still waiting to receive.... *immortality*. She was a vampire.

Vampires can't have children so the only logical explanation was that Mr. Bechard turned her around the time he initially became one.

A lump in my throat was giving me difficulties to breathe. I almost ran to the bathroom because even though I was under the clear sky, I felt like suffocating.

I filled my hands with cool water and washed my makeup away in a desperate need to extinguish the fire that I felt forming inside me. The feeling was so intense that I was afraid the day when I set the bedsheets on fire would repeat itself with a much higher intensity.

I remained there for a while with my head bowed in front of the sink, trying to collect myself.

When I finally gathered the strength to look in the mirror, I recognized the face I saw every day. A face that is getting older. For many people, it wouldn't be of great importance but a few months ago I noticed a fine wrinkle forming on my forehead. This was a message to me; *I was running out of time.*

A few minutes later Damien came in with a worried look all over his face.

"Take me home," where the only words I managed to say.

In a few moments we were in his car, less than a half an hour to the safety of his apartment.

For the first time in three years, I wanted to be alone.

The truth is, when I found out that Adam had turned Lala I had felt a hint of jealousy as Damien was delaying this moment for me.

I secretly waited every night hoping that he would do it. I used to tell myself *maybe on our anniversary, maybe on my birthday... maybe on Christmas* but years flew by and that *maybe* never came.

What worried me most was the fact that when I tried, on countless occasions, to think back to our earlier conversations, he never said he'd do it.

I almost became obsessed with this idea. Around a year ago I asked him to turn me. That was somehow my final hope, that he was expecting me to ask him, to be ready... but he refused me. He told me that *he* wasn't ready and asked me for patience.

I accepted his decision for that moment, but time wasn't on my side anymore. I couldn't wait for him to turn me when I'm 40.

I never lacked self-esteem and I know my face is more than

pleasing to the eye, my fight was keeping it that way. This is bound to happen anyway. I had no doubt that he loved me, so why wouldn't it happen at the right time so I could be at ease with myself?

"Sarah?!" he whispered, kneeling in front of me as I sat motionlessly on the couch. He took my hands into his own and tried to decipher what was wrong with me.

"I'm running out of time Damien, I want you to turn me." I didn't have the patience for diplomacy tonight.

"We've talked about this before," he muttered, getting up and stepped back slightly from me.

"You said you weren't ready, but I feel you're not telling me the truth." I raised my voice at him for the first time.

"You're right. The truth is Sarah, I don't plan on turning you."

"What?!" I could feel my heart pounding in my throat as everything I used to know was collapsing right in front of me.

"Why did you ask me to have patience then?!"

"I'll explain," he said with a sad tone and took a place on the couch next to me.

"I didn't lie. I wasn't ready back then. You see, there's a fine line between drinking, turning and killing someone.

When you drink, you can have around a liter without endangering the human, but when you turn someone you have to almost drain them but stop right before their heart stops beating.

I said that I'm not ready because I'm personally so attached to you and the line gets blurry when this happens.

I wasn't sure I could stop. I'm still not sure.... I've failed-" his eyes turned cold and his desperation for blood was oblivious so I let him have a glass so he could gather his thoughts and continue our conversation.

"The more I thought about it, the more I realized that I don't want and can't trust myself to turn you.

I love you and I don't want this for you.

Mortality has its beauty because you get to cherish every second you have. I realized that once again because of you. Because *I cherish* every second with you."

"I don't want mortality. I want you for eternity not just for a few years"- I was almost pleading him.

"But I don't want this for you. To have to hide from the light, never be able to feel the sun on your skin and have you live forever in the shadows. I already regret you doing it because of me.

This is a curse!

I can't let it happen to you. I won't allow it!"

"Then explain to me how all of this will work. Do you expect me to grow old next to you?"

"Yes. I want to remember and worship every moment we ever spend together and I'll love you equally throughout eternity. I'm doing this because I love you... *I can't doom you just because I love you.*"

"**To remember**, Damien... You want to *remember* me?! What life would you think I'll have, growing old while you'll remain forever young?"

"The way your body looks has no importance to me. I will love every one of your wrinkles," he smiled, trying to ease our argument.

"But I won't. I will hate myself and eventually you... and I don't want that."

"This decision wasn't easy for me to make either. I'm the one who will live throughout eternity without you.

Can't you see that no matter what I choose, *I'll end up losing*?"

"You made a decision regarding my life without even consulting me!

I really think you're afraid of committing to someone for an eternity."

"You know that's not true."

"You claim you don't want to curse me to a life of darkness, but you're really cursing me to a life without you.

Goodbye, Damien!"

Dangerous plan

I packed a few of my things and he didn't even try to stop me. I knew from the start he wouldn't. He respected my decision the way he expected me to respect his. The only difference between us was that I couldn't. I couldn't live, just waiting to die beside him.

I knew what he meant by being forced to live in the darkness. For me, it was my option, my decision to choose to be close to Damien. It wasn't imposed like it is for him. I could feel his suffering over time. I was aware of it since that day he spent in my apartment. He even told me stories about how he was hunted, forced to hide on so many occasions.

From his point of view, he was right, but from my point of view, I was right too.

I left his apartment without being able to look him in the eyes, shutting a door behind me that every fiber in me begged to *keep open.*

In a weird way, I really believed that he was somehow afraid to commit. No matter how much he loves me, *eternity is a long time.*

I didn't check myself in a five stars hotel but returned to my old apartment. Maybe I'm sentimental, but the nights spent there waiting for Damien's soul to visit me never let me give it up. A couple of years ago I managed to buy it from the guy I used to pay rent to.

I didn't know exactly what to do with myself, I think I remained in front of the window with tears streaming down my face for hour after hour until the dawns light came.

I cursed the rays of light that were making their way between the buildings and at one point hated light itself. It was my first step in choosing *darkness.*

A year later

I didn't leave New York because I had nowhere else to go. Europe was our playground, but never my home. It was a place where my most painful memories lived and I could hardly get by as things are in NY.

My gallery became the most famous in The Big Apple, maybe even the states, but I didn't care. In what Damien had wanted for me most I was failing miserably to do... *live.*

I was in a numb state, like a walking cadaver that waited for something that will never come. He would never be mine again.

I used to tell myself so many times that I could live without him, but I never actually believed it. There was a hole in my heart that was bringing me closer to madness each day.

I was hurt and desperate, unable to come to peace with my life. I decided to pay Lala a visit. She had tried to contact me several times, but I couldn't deal with anyone else and just wanted to be left alone. To be honest, after I broke off with Damien, I didn't leave my apartment for over a month. I still don't go out except for occasional walks during the night. I guess that at an unconscious level I keep waiting for a creature of the dark to find me, turn me or kill me, just end my misery.

I put on one of my old dresses, noticing how it hung loosely on me, then turned to the mirror to put a little makeup on a face I barely recognized.

It was like I was split in two, one part of me was still here, but the other half, the part that held my power to be happy... that, I left behind with him... Damien.

I left my apartment at dusk and a cab took me to the alley near Adam's place. I hadn't spoken with people, except through emails, in so long that the driver's questions were making me uncomfortable. He was just being polite but this made me realize that I was beginning to develop a phobia of being out of the house.

As soon as he stopped, I paid him. From the corner of my eye I noticed a familiar face descending the stairs to the club. Joseph, a person I would have feared a while ago, but who now had no effect on me at all.

I took the stairs up to Adam's loft and after passing the long hallway knocked on the door.

Lala answered, a shocked look appeared on her face but was quickly replaced by a friendly hug.

She looked at me with *a sorrow that hurt,* then invited me in. Lala apologized that she can't serve me with anything as they don't usually eat or drink. She was definitely not expecting my company. I laughed in my mind because Adam was finally succeeding in emancipating her a little. The old Laura couldn't care less what politeness meant.

She tried to have a conversation, but all of her questions were turning into short answers from me, followed by awkward moments of silence. She spoke about their lives a little. They were really happy together and you could clearly see that from the way she talked, but I couldn't listen for long until a knot clenched in my abdomen. I felt like I was just one step away from throwing up. It wasn't jealousy, it was regret for the life I should've had.

I think she thought that I was uneasy so, she changed the subject, telling me about the club and her daily activities.

Adam showed up and was also surprised to see me here. Although Lala asked me all kinds of questions, she never asked me the essential one "What brings you by?" Adam instead made sure to ask that one.

I looked at them both and with all the power left in me I looked at Lala and spoke "I came here for you to turn me."

I could see from her eyes that she didn't know what to say, unsure what answer to give me.

I kept my eyes on Lala, studying her mimic, hoping for her to agree until Adam intervened "You know he would kill her if she would, don't you?"... and the truth was that I didn't. It didn't come to my mind, not even for a second, that his interdiction still applied. It seemed like something from lifetimes ago.

"I don't think he even cares," I said with despise, but deep down I was hoping to get information. I never heard from him since the night I left.

"He cares, Sarah. He's not well either. He's locked himself in the French chateau for the last year. But believe me, if anything were to happen to you, he wouldn't stand by and do nothing. He would kill me or Lala without blinking." The rest of what he said were just words that floated in the air without reaching my ears to understand them.

I kept thinking how I hoped that one night I'd venture into an alley dark enough to meet my end or my new beginning. Damien's interdiction was ruining that for me too.

"I have to go." I got up and rushed to the door in a desperate attempt to find the last reason for living... *a hope that my life would be as I imagined.*

"Will you come back and visit me soon?" she called after me.

"Yes" I lied in the hopes that she wouldn't follow me, because in reality, I had no idea what tomorrow may bring.

I descended the stairs but didn't stop at the ground level, instead I went into the club.

As the door opened all eyes were on me. I walked past a few of them and headed towards the center of the room.

With each step, I noticed how they were getting further from me, as if I carried a plague.

I approached the bar and all the seats emptied, draining all the drops of patience left in me "Are you all so afraid of him?!" my voice echoed through their ears and made some of them head through the door. I guess that was my answer.

There was no point in being there, so I went out into the alley, trying to figure out a way to get home.

I was looking at my phone when a cold chill hit me as a dangerous creature made its way behind my back.

I should run, be scared, but tonight it didn't give me any of those feelings, it gave me hope.

"Joseph," I whispered before turning, then I shifted my body and let his cold look meet mine.

"Were you expecting me?" he smirked analyzing me from head to toe.

"Yes" I could barely hide my joy.

"I know why you're here," he whispered, pushing me into a dark corner.

"I've been thinking about you since that night when I tasted you...hmmm...the pleasure you brought me," he growled, placing a hand on my hip.

"You can have more than just a quick taste tonight," I whispered back, close to his trembling lips that were barely able to conceal his fangs.

"I would like nothing more than that, but unfortunately I wouldn't live long enough to enjoy it. You see I don't worry about Damien's wrath, but for what the fear that he instilled in the other vampires can do," he whispered, letting his hand fall on my thigh.

"I guess you're no use to me then," I growled, taking his hand off me and nearly breaking one of his fingers.

"How did you -" was all I managed to hear as I walked further down the street so I could find a cab.

After half an hour I reached my apartment and went straight into the kitchen to pour myself a drink. I needed something to numb my senses, at least for a while, to make me forget for a second that he was once mine.

I reached the fridge and the only alcohol I could find was a new vodka bottle. I took it out and tried to open the seal but it was glued to tightly on the cap, so I reached a fruit knife from the counter but in my rush grazed the tip of my finger.

It was a small cut, but a few drops of the red liquid made their way out, giving birth to a very *dangerous plan.*

Nothing

I checked myself in the mirror for the thousandth time, rearranging my red dress so that every fold of the material fell perfectly into place. I hadn't worn heels in a while so my feet were already killing me, but I didn't have time to complain. With my hair carefully arranged in a loose bun and my makeup just finished, I was ready.

I looked just like a countess that has lost her way through the back of time, but now was going home.

I rented a limo to take me from my hotel to my destination for the night. As dusk was setting, I embarked on my voyage.

After almost an hour's drive, the car pulled to a stop in front of a large metal gate.

I got out and signaled the driver to leave, then walked past the security guard and into the garden.

I cursed as my heels got caught in some of the pavement, but finally reached the front door with my shoes still intact.

I grabbed the door handle but it was locked, so I found myself forced to knock. I felt bitter about that in a way.

After a few minutes of being left to wait in the cold outside, the door opened and an old woman dressed in black appeared in front of me.

"I was freezing outside." I muttered as I entered without asking permission.

"Where is he?" I asked, looking over her shoulder since she was still standing in my way.

"Mr. Arion isn't in!" she said still not wanting to budge.

"Lies. Move Margaret before I'll throw you outside and lock the door." I growled until I could read the fear in her eyes.

"Which room?" I snapped, already searching five chambers on that level.

She didn't answer, just stood in the hallway and gave me a defying look.

I could feel my forces gathering with a wrath unknown to me until a week ago. My conscience wasn't my own anymore but shaded by a hint of madness.

"Here," a voice snapped me back to reality before I made a move I might regret.

Tears started rolling on my face even though I promised myself I'd stay strong.

I ran to him and his arms wrapped around me the second we made contact, burying his face in my hair.

We didn't move for minutes, maybe hours, like stone statues who wished time would stand still for them.

"You came back," he finally whispered and I parted just a few inches to be able to look in his eyes.

For the first time, I saw weakness like someone made a magic spell and said the right words to crush him. I could see that he was suffering not only from his gaze but also from his slack look. His hair that used to be carefully arranged was messy now, his clothes were randomly selected and the small stumble I used to love was almost turning into a beard.

I searched his lips, listening to the faded crack of all humanity left in me.

"I want to stay," I murmured, trembling in his arms. He didn't answer but kissed me harder with such passion and intensity that I could feel his poisonous fangs scratch my lips.

I didn't back down but pulled him closer, then in the next second, he was gone.

I knew where he was going, so I followed unhurriedly. Tonight, I had all the time in the world.

Numbness, determination, or madness... I'm not sure which one of these I was anymore, but with each stair I climbed, some unearthly force was pushing me towards him.

I opened the door to his office and found him in an armchair with an almost empty blood bottle.

"I'm sorry, I guess I lost training. I was unprepared," he spoke with a more powerful voice.

He got up and approached me and rested his palm on the side of my face, brushing his thumb on my bottom lip. "You look astonishing," he whispered, mesmerized again for a split second. He then looked down at himself and probably realized how this year had changed him.

He went to the cabinet and pulled out a bottle of wine, opened it, then poured me a glass.

"I leave you in its company for a few minutes. I promise I'll be quick," he was gone in an instant.

I needed the alcohol as much as he needed the drink, so before he could return, I was on my third glass.

I heard the door crack open and realized that someone from my past has returned. The old Damien was there standing in front of me, freshly shaven, with flawlessly brushed hair and a black dress shirt that left his neck tattoo to peek out from under it.

I felt like that evening at the Gala when I first saw him. My emotions were barely controlling themselves and for a moment I was that weak Sarah again, dominated by his unspoken words, letting myself drift off in a dream that is long forgotten.

He grinned, knowing the effect he still held on me and almost in slow motion approached me.

"You're cold", he noticed, letting one of his palms gently stroke my arm.

I can't tell if it was from the uneasy state I was in, though probably more strongly related to the tiredness I had collecting over the last year. It was maybe just because the room temperature was below 20°C and I was wearing a sleeves dress, but I was shivering.

Damien didn't need heat as humans do and even though his senses are ultra-sensitive, he never cared about temperatures except for when I was around.

Since the chateau was built around the 15th century, it had stoves when we first moved in. These were replaced with a much more advanced central heating system. The problem with this was that it took almost a day from when you started it to when it could properly heat the estate. Damien shortly figured out a solution and grabbing our glasses, showing me into one of those great chambers we had upstairs.

This was one of the few rooms that had a fireplace, so he grabbed an armchair for me and brought it in front of the fire inviting me to sit. He then arranged a blanket over my shoulders.

As soon as I was settled, he lit the fire. My thoughts raced towards the memories of the nights we got lost in each other's company in front of the orange flames.

Soon, I was starting to relax, receiving my oh so needed heat. Over time I think I started to despise humankind, especially its poorly constructed wrapping. This flesh that gets sick and ages, rushing your end when your spirit is built to go on for eternities.

After setting the fire, Damien remained on a rug that laid in front of the fireplace, studying me with an uncommon joy, but also like he was trying to immortalize each one of my features in his mind.

I think he couldn't help himself because after a few moments he asked "Are you here to stay?"

I could feel the distress in his voice as he was hoping for a positive answer, but I needed to make sure for a final time "Yes. But do you want me for a lifetime of for eternity?"

"Sarah..." he replied with the same tone as he did that night a year ago. *Nothing has changed.*

"Please believe me that an eternity is worth less than a lifetime. I want you to shiver when it's cold and be able to get drunk on that wine while you sunbathe in the garden. You have no idea how little things are considered great gifts in my world." He spoke with a concerned tone as I was just about to walk away from him again ... but not this time. This time I'm here until the *end.*

"It's ok. I got accustomed to the idea. That's why I'm here today... I'm here today because *I don't want to live without you.*"

He left his spot and knelt in front of my armchair, wrapping his arms around me "then you understand that it's not because I'm afraid of commitment. I just fear of that time when days will start repeating themselves and you'll also see this as a curse. I don't want to doom you to this."

"I know." I looked at him hungrily, but at the same time I was lying to him. I wanted so badly for the days to repeat themselves so that I can meet his lips in an eternal kiss and our nights of passion could turn into decades.

"*Mine,*" he growled, crushing his lips on mine and sending shivers throughout my body.

Somehow, he was in control again and didn't even look at the bottle that was now empty.

"Wait," I murmured getting down from the chair to join him on the floor.

I started unbuttoning his shirt so that my lips could trace the ink on his skin. I took the path of his neck then descended to his chest. A long growl escaped his throat and his hand wrapped in my hair, lifting me up a little so he could find my lips again.

My thighs fastened around his waist while he was slowly descending to my collarbone. He always liked to spend a few more moments there, I think it has something to do with his animalistic nature and the need to be close to the blood that runs throughout me, but tonight this was *a fatal mistake*. As his tongue roamed my skin. I took out the same small fruit knife that I found in the kitchen a week ago and that I had carefully hidden between the plies of my dress, in an instant making a small cut on my neck, inches away from his lips.

No amount of blood glasses could have ever prepared him for this. Damien has disappeared and left me with *his monster*. ***Exactly as I planned.***

His fangs pierced my skin and I could hear the sound of my flesh cracking, followed by the most agonizing pain.

For a brief second a self-defense mechanism created by my unnatural powers kicked in, but I pushed it back with all force I had inside. There was no way back. *I had no more time.*

I felt him drinking of me and his grip getting tighter with every single sip until I felt almost drained.

He had to stop before there was nothing left, so I just had to push him back.

I didn't take something into consideration.

As my powers left me, they were becoming **his own** and now I was defenseless in front of the *vampire*.

In my final attempt to escape, I dug my nails so hard into his back that I could feel his skin tearing under them as I scratched deeply into his flesh. In an instant, a horrified look appeared on his face. Damien was coming back, but in his fight to regain control he took an involuntary breath that extracted the very last precious drops of blood I had in me.

My eyes felt like mountains had sat upon them. As they closed, the final image etched on my mind was that of horror and fear written across his face. I drifted away between his screams to a senseless place, a place I didn't belong yet, but still, here I was surrounded by darkness until there was *nothing*.

The Sin of You

Epilogue

"Everything is more beautiful because we're doomed. You will never be lovelier than you are now. We will never be here again" - Homer.

Damien *-earlier that evening*

I stood still waiting for the darkness to fully take its rightful place between the hills that surrounded my estate, as I did every evening for the past year. Only tonight was different. I could feel it. Something was waiting for me as fate has cast its final joke upon me.

My gut didn't betray me and in less than an hour I felt her warm presence. I watched surprised as she got out of the car and made her way to the front door as if the last year hadn't happened.

I could hear her shouting at Margaret with a hint of madness in her voice that I chose to ignore.

Her heels were making a loud sound as her steps were hurrying to find me- "Here," I called out to her, still unsure if this was just an ephemeral dream.

She ran towards me in tears and my arms grabbed her in a frantic need to feel her close to me once again. I couldn't let her go, still surprised, but drunken by her presence.

"You came back," I couldn't hide my enthusiasm and as soon as I noticed her approaching lips, found her in a kiss.

"I want to stay," she whispered while I could feel her shaking. In my anguish to take her pain upon me, I kissed her so intensely that my body betrayed me and let my fangs almost graze her.

I stopped in time and almost teleported to my office upstairs, devouring a whole bottle of blood before she could follow my steps.

"I'm sorry, I guess I lost training. I was unprepared," I spoke as she entered the room. I managed to regain my strengths since her presence took me by surprise and my self-control deteriorated throughout the last year.

I finally found the stability to get near her again and caressed her face, stroking her bottom lip with my thumb.

She was astonishing and I had to let her know, but I quickly realized that my own aspect had nothing in common anymore with the man she used to know.

I offered her a glass of wine, excused myself and went straight to the bathroom to shave and arrange my messy hair, then I changed my white unbuttoned shirt with a black dress shirt. She deserved the best possible version of me and I wasn't going to fail her.

Her eyes shimmered as I entered the room and the memory of the night we first met came alive.

She was still the most beautiful woman I ever knew and our connection felt even stronger than before.

I touched her arm, but she was so cold. I realized that the room was unheated even though it was late October.

I don't need heat and Margaret only turned it on in the east wing where she usually stays. I used to check the temperature on reflex while Sarah lived here, but I guess I numbed that too.

I guided her towards one of the great chambers where we had a fireplace. This was actually a dining room back in the days, but we used it as a *recreation* room, spending hours *entangled* in front of the dancing flames.

After a few moments, the room became a little warmer, so I took a place on the rug in front of her still wondering if fate was finally smiling on me.

She was breathtaking, dressed with a red gown that wrapped

around her body and showing each one of her curves. In a way, I wished I could keep her forever like this, but *I had no right too*. She would eventually despise me and I can't survive with such a thought.

She will always be like this for me. As gorgeous as she is in this fading moment, I'll cherish every second she's willing to give me for the rest of my existence.

I needed a certitude, an answer to the question that had troubled me from the instant I felt her presence "Are you here to stay?"

"Yes. But do you want me for a lifetime of for eternity?", she answered back.

I wanted to choose *eternity* so badly, but not with the curse it brought.

To be honest, I have an ulterior reason for my rejection. It had also to do with me failing a long time ago in a past reddened with the blood of my enemies.

I was lost, almost fully submerged in dark forces, just one step from ending mankind when I met my savior. A girl with a soul so pure that she awoke me from my bloodbaths and showed me the real values of humanity.

I had forgotten how it felt to be human...what it really meant to be human. She showed me step by step the beauty in her gentleness, how to really appreciate life, the value of a second when your time is counted.

I don't know if I loved her or carried a great deal of gratitude, compared to Sarah I think it wasn't love.

I wanted to do something in return, to keep her with me even though I was going to take her gifts and give her a curse. She tried to explain, but I was a vampire and she was in love. I didn't even need the power of conviction to get her to agree, she would have done anything I wanted.

Without realizing that I was only satisfying my selfish needs, I bit her, drinking her sweet blood until she was one step away from turning. But I was blind... Unprepared and still with the taste of the war lingering in my veins, I sipped too much and she didn't come back to me. She was just an empty vessel that used to shelter a soul that I *unwillingly* betrayed.

This is one of the reasons I can't turn Sarah. Her blood is too sweet not only for me but for any vampire. I felt it since that night at The Count. At first, I thought I was wrong because she was my half and I started to think it only has an effect on me. But I saw it in Joseph's eyes that night, in his desperation for more.

I won't change my previous decision even though I risk her leaving me again. I won't jeopardize the beautiful years she has ahead just to doom her.

"Sarah...Please believe me that eternity is worth less than a life-time. I want you to shiver when it's cold and be able to get drunk on that wine while you sunbathe in the garden. You have no idea how little things are considered great gifts in my world." I tried explaining once again.

"It's ok. I got accustomed to the idea. That's why I'm here today... I'm here today because I don't want to live without you." I should have seen it coming, but she was feeding my ears with the lies they were hungry to hear.

I reached her and enclosed my arms around her arms "You understand that it's not because I'm afraid of commitment. I just fear of that time when days will start repeating themselves and you'll also see this as a curse. I don't want to doom you to this."

It hurt me that even for a moment she thought my love wasn't strong enough to last through all eternity.

"I know," she *confirmed* that she finally understood me and was willing to accept our lifetime together.

"*Mine!*" I roared as the outside world was just spinning around us, crushing my lips on hers, numbing all instincts, and almost willingly falling into a trap.

"Wait," she whispered lowering herself on the floor to join me.

She removed my shirt, letting her lips descending on my chest, drugging the man inside me. Her movement on my skin was delicious. For a second, I almost lost it and began thinking about reaching for another bottle, but I could bear no interruption.

During the years spent together, I had started not needing the blood while spending the nights with her. With my hands entangled in her hair I brought her back to my lips and convinced myself that my composure could be contained at the right level as long as I was the one in control.

I had no idea how wrong I was. From the second she entered the room she was *the only one pulling the strings*.

She wrapped her legs around me, pressing firmly on my manhood, weakening me even more.

I started kissing her so passionately, making up for all the lost time, then descended, letting my lips feast on her neckline.

I felt her move but was convinced that she was just rearranging her dress that was now in the way. Without a warning, the smell of blood filled my nostrils, so close to my mouth that my fangs emerged in an instant. Even though I tried to fight the monster inside, it could not be stopped this time.

Everything went blank for a few moments and woke up with excruciating pain in my back, but before I could find out the origin of it, I was petrified at what was happening. My fangs had pierced Sarah's flesh while my whole body overflowed with a bizarre power.

I backed off, horrified at what was happening, but it was too late. The drop of blood that I felt shaking on my fangs was her last.

Desperate, I bit her again, trying to put the tiny drops back in her body. It was all in vain... *My screams, my curses...my prayers were all in vain.*

A sensation of vomit took control and I knew in that instant that everything is lost. *I was lost.* More powerful but also weaker than ever, I was now holding inside me a special part of her. A gift I neither wanted nor plan to ever use.

I was reliving a nightmare of much greater proportions, overtaken by feelings that were tormenting my soul, draining me of all humanity and turning me into the monster I really am... *The monster that killed her.*

I stayed there for days, holding her fragile body in my arms and unable to decide which moment should be the last when I will feel her close.

I couldn't let anyone touch her even as my feet battled to carry her to the crypt. It felt like walking on spines, paying with the pain of my soul crushing with every step I took towards her tomb.

I pulled the cap, unable to look at what I did anymore, falling on my knees crushed by the weight of invisible walls that were plunging on me.

My life became *darkness*, pure rage pounding in all of my body while feeling that I'm drowning with each new second.

Fate had its will, taking from me the greatest price for this life. Doomed to forever roam this earth haunted by her memory, feeding with each day on my sparkles of humanity until there will be nothing left.

Nothing comes for free and this was the toll I had to pay for my immortality.

Killing an angel to fulfill a prophecy, letting "**the sin of you** linger on my mind in the eternity of time."

Special thanks to my friend and book editor, Richard.

Made in the USA
Middletown, DE
08 November 2020

23572331R00124